THE CHERRY VALLEY MIDDLE SCHOOL NEWS

# DEAR KNOW-IT-ALL!

# Breaking News

by RACHEL WISE

Simon Spotlight
New York  London  Toronto  Sydney  New Delhi

**SIMON SPOTLIGHT**
An imprint of Simon & Schuster Children's Publishing Division
1230 Avenue of the Americas, New York, New York 10020
Copyright © 2013 by Simon & Schuster, Inc. All rights reserved, including the right of reproduction in whole or in part in any form.
SIMON SPOTLIGHT and colophon are registered trademarks of Simon & Schuster, Inc.
Text by Sheila Sweeny Higginson

For information about special discounts for bulk purchases, please contact Simon & Schuster Special Sales at 1-866-506-1949 or business@simonandschuster.com.
Manufactured in the United States of America 1013 OFF
First Edition 10 9 8 7 6 5 4 3 2 1
ISBN 978-1-4424-8964-6 (pbk)
ISBN 978-1-4424-8965-3 (hc)
ISBN 978-1-4424-8966-0 (eBook)
Library of Congress Control Number 2013946535

# Chapter 1

## FOOTBALL SEASON BEGINS; MARTONE FALLS FOR STAR QUARTERBACK

★ ★ ★

If you're a fact-loving person like I am, you probably think superstitions are a little silly. So tell me, why does it seem like *everyone* believes in them? Take my mom, for instance. You would think that a freelance accountant, a person who works with numbers all day, would know that there's nothing particularly special or spooky about the number thirteen. Except that every time the calendar shows a big black thirteen on a Friday, Mom gets an uneasy look in her eye. It's like she's waiting for something really bad to happen. Of course nothing does, just like nearly every other day of the year!

As a journalist, my instincts are to get to

the truth of the matter. So I started Googling, and I found some interesting information about "friggatriskaidekaphobia." (That's the actual term for the condition of the fear of Friday the thirteenth. And I dare you to say that three times fast!) Did you know that in Spanish-speaking countries, it's Tuesday the thirteenth that's considered unlucky? And in Italy, Friday the seventeenth is the day of doom. I figure that kind of info will come in handy when I'm traveling the world on assignment as an investigative reporter.

But the next step on my career path is to continue to build my reputation as star reporter of the *Cherry Valley Voice*, our school newspaper. Of course, I don't usually fly solo. Mr. Trigg likes to give the best articles to his dream team, his "Woodward and Bernstein," as he calls Michael Lawrence and me, after the *Washington Post*'s legendary reporting duo. I'm not sure we'll ever get behind the scenes at the White House, but we did write the story that revealed the truth about our class president contenders.

Not that I'm complaining about sharing the glory. Not one teensy bit. I won't even mind if someday Michael and I get picked to be coeditors in chief. Then I'll get to work side by side with him *all* the time. I've known Michael since kindergarten, and even though he sometimes annoyingly calls me Pasty (you eat paste one time when you're five and you're branded forever!), he's still the only boy I've ever dreamed of calling my boyfriend.

How can I describe Michael Lawrence's insane cuteness to you? Let's just say that if you took the hottest member of every boy band, mixed up all of their best qualities in a pot, and then increased them to the tenth power, well, then you'd have Michael Lawrence. It's actually shocking that he hasn't been discovered yet, now that I think about it. ***Popular Athlete/Reporter Leaves Cherry Valley for World Tour.*** As if! Of course, I don't really know if he sings. He definitely doesn't dance (I've seen him!), and I'm not sure that he plays an instrument, so I don't know what he'd actually do on tour. Probably just look cute. Luckily, Michael has many other talents, including writing, sports, and making the best cinnamon buns I've ever tasted. Maybe someone on a cooking show could draft him. He'd make such a dreamy host. I know I'd watch him. Anyway, I'm surprised someone hasn't offered something to him to make him a star.

One offer that I couldn't turn down was continuing to write the Dear Know-It-All column for the *Voice*. Dear Know-It-All is the advice column that I write secretly. No one, not even my BFF, Hailey Jones, knows that I'm Know-It-All. It's cool, but it's kind of stressful, too. Mr. Trigg caught me off guard when he offered me a second year of the secret assignment. And considering all the drama from last year—like, "Hello, cyber stalker!"—I definitely have had some doubts about the job. Sometimes giving advice is really hard and I'm just not sure what to tell people to do. Like right now, I can't even decide what to wear to Cherry Valley's first game of the football season. And since Michael Lawrence is the all-star quarterback, this is a very crucial decision!

So back to superstitions: I don't have many, being a believer in cold, hard facts, but I do have a lucky green T-shirt. (Its luck is based on the fact that it is the exact same shade of green as my eyes.) Maybe it's not really lucky, but it does make me really happy. I put it on with a long hippy skirt and green UGGs. I wrapped a sparkly beaded scarf around my neck. Then I threw on an armful of bangle bracelets and some beaded hanging earrings for a little extra pizzazz. I looked in the mirror. *Not bad, Martone*, I thought to myself.

But the real proof waited across the hallway. I knocked on my sister Allie's door. Allie can be a real pain because she's always creeping around my stuff, but she does have much better fashion sense than I do.

"What do you think?" I asked as I warily entered her room.

Allie glanced up from her texting for exactly one one-hundredth of a second and rolled her eyes. "No," she huffed, obviously revolted by my choice of apparel. "Just no."

"But it's my lucky shirt," I explained.

"Lucky because you're going to fold it up and put it back in your drawer," Allie said bluntly. "And that scarf? That jewelry? You do realize you're going to a football game, right?"

Allie took my hand and led me back into my room the way she used to drag me across the street when I was too little to cross by myself. She opened my closet door and started picking out items and throwing them onto my bed.

"Allie, I don't have a lot of time to try on clothes," I complained. "Hailey will be here any minute!"

Like I mentioned before, Hailey is my best friend forever—yin to my yang. But if you didn't know us well, you might think we have absolutely nothing in common. She can juggle a soccer ball effortlessly. I have trouble making it down the stairs without falling flat on my face. I get my highest marks in language arts. Hailey's dyslexia makes reading and writing challenging for her. Hailey's happy in sweats and her soccer team jersey, and she always looks great in them too. I like to look a little more put together. At least, I try.

But as Allie was so kind to point out, I can just as easily fail, too.

"This won't take long," Allie said. "Just listen. You're the starting QB's girlfriend. You have to look great, but not like you're trying too hard. Think casual chic."

"I'm not Michael Lawrence's girlfriend!" I said automatically. Well, I didn't think I was. But I'd like to be.

"Whatever." Allie snorted. "Just take my advice."

I flopped onto my bed and put my hands over my face. Allie mumbled to herself as she threw different combinations of clothes together. I looked at the clock, and my stomach started to hurt. How could getting dressed for a football game be so incredibly painful?

"Try this," Allie said as she tossed some clothes my way.

I quickly pulled on some black leggings and then a miniskirt. Next came a gray tank, followed by a silver sweater and a black blazer. A pair of old-school black high-top sneakers finished the outfit. I looked in the mirror and smiled. I looked very casual and comfy but very stylish, too. Allie was amazing—the outfit worked like a lucky charm. Just in time, too.

"*Saaaammmm!*" I heard Hailey call from the front door.

"*Commminnngggg!*" I yelled back. "Thanks, Allie!" I called behind me, but she had already started texting again.

I raced down the stairs (without tripping!) and stopped to say good-bye to my mom. She was in her home office, intently focused on some confusing jumble of budget numbers.

"You look great," she said, making me wonder if I should go back upstairs and change back into my lucky shirt.

"Thanks," I answered. "Go, Cherry Valley!"

"Go, Cherry Valley?" Hailey said from behind my back. "More like Go, Sam! Supercute outfit!"

"Yeah, it was Allie's creation," I confessed reluctantly.

"She got her fashion sense from me," Mom said, not even kidding.

"Right," Hailey and I said at exactly the same time.

We raced out of the house and jumped into the backseat of Hailey's car. Hailey's dad turned around and pretended to tip his hat.

"Good evening, mademoiselles," he said in a fake accent. "Where shall I be driving you this fine afternoon?"

Hailey and I just looked at each other and started to giggle uncontrollably. Parents. Did they even have a clue how embarrassing they could be?

"Football field, Dad," Hailey answered as soon as she had regained her composure. "Pronto."

★　★　★

It took only seven minutes to get from my house to the football field, but in that short period of time, Hailey bombarded me with at least ten thousand questions. *Did Michael say anything about hanging out with you after the game? Do you think the guys from the team will go to Scoops? Should we go too? What if they have a bad game? Do you know if that cute guy from West Hills plays football? Do you think he has a girlfriend?*

"Hailey, stop!" I said. "We're just going to watch a football game. The rest we'll improvise. Okay?"

"Okay." Hailey laughed. "I have just one last question for you, Samantha Martone." Hailey coughed and attempted to put on an I'm-being-incredibly-serious expression. Then she held up her hand to my face like she was holding a microphone. "Will . . . you . . . touch . . . ," she asked, sounding like the most dramatic sports reporter ever, ". . . the cougar?"

We both started giggling uncontrollably.

"Yes, I guess I will," I confessed. "I'll bow to peer pressure and silly superstition."

"It's not silly," Hailey said. "It's tradition. And really, really bad luck if you don't."

Let me explain. There's a statue of a cougar standing on its hind legs in front of Cherry Valley Middle School. All of our sports teams are named the Cougars, and like a million years ago, some class raised enough money to have the statue built and installed in front of the school. Hailey's soccer team, Michael's baseball and football teams, bowling, tennis, they're all Cougars. Even our robotics team.

Cherry Valley legend says that if you rub the cougar's paw, you'll have good luck. Everyone at Cherry Valley Middle School seems to believe this myth—students, parents, teachers, even Principal Pfeiffer. Kids rub Mr. Cougar's paw before a big test, when they're going to ask someone to a school dance, and of course, before every sporting event. The paw has been rubbed so many times over the years that it is as smooth and shiny as glass.

When we turned the last corner, I felt a little flutter in my stomach. Even though Michael Lawrence is definitely *not* my boyfriend—yet—it was going to be fun to cheer for him. And the weather was perfect for football. I looked out the window and started to daydream. The clear blue skies; the red, yellow, and brown leaves that swirled in the wind; the crisp chill in the air—it was the perfect setting for a girl reporter to walk home hand in hand with the triumphant quarterback after the game. *Ace Reporter Spotted with Handsome All-Star QB!*

"Sam!" Hailey said, a little too loudly considering we were sitting right next to each other. "What do you think is going on?"

It took me a second to realize what Hailey was talking about. She pointed out her window at the front of our school. A large crowd was gathered.

"Wow, it looks like everyone is really into football this year," Hailey's dad noted.

It didn't make a lot of sense to me. If they were coming to see the game, why weren't they heading to the football field?

Then we spotted the police car. This was definitely not a pregame pep rally. I glanced at Hailey, and she looked as nervous as I felt. Why would the police be at a middle school football game?

"You two stay here while I make sure everything's okay," Hailey's dad said.

Hailey and I held hands until her dad waved us over. As we made our way through the parking lot, it seemed like everyone from school was there. We had to weave our way through the crowd that was circled around the front of the school, and it felt like we were never going to get there. But we did. And then we finally saw what all the commotion was about.

It was Mr. Cougar. His paw was on the ground, smashed into tiny pieces. His body was covered with a spray-painted message: *CV—Your Luck Has Run Out.* Police were wrapping yellow caution tape around the statue. Lots of people were taking pictures of the vandalized property. It seemed like a scene from a movie, not like something that would happen in our town.

Hailey gasped. "Cherry Valley Middle School is doomed."

# Chapter 2

## CHERRY VALLEY MAKES THE NEWS!

★ ★ ★

You know that awkward moment when you realize that everyone is feeling one way and you're feeling something completely different? Like when there's a particularly gruesome part in a scary movie that makes the whole audience in the theater gasp, but you laugh out loud because the special effects seem so cheesy? That's kind of the moment I was having when I heard Hailey gasp.

Don't get me wrong. There wasn't *anything* funny about what had happened to Mr. Cougar. It's just that while everyone else in the crowd looked shocked or upset or worried, my Spidey Senses started tingling. Of course, by Spidey Senses, I mean my reporter's instincts. There are lots of things I know I still need to work on, like choosing outfits for football games and navigating the stairs without tripping. But I am super confident in my ability to sniff out news, and this was the most newsworthy event to happen at our school since I started working on the *Cherry Valley Voice*. I could feel the excitement pumping through my veins. I knew there was someone else who would feel the same way—Michael Lawrence. He was probably in the locker room listening to his coach pump up the team with an inspirational pre-game speech, though.

Just then I heard Gregory Toms yell, "Hey, everyone, the game is still on!" The corners of Hailey's mouth turned up ever so slightly. If you were anyone but her best friend who happens to be a reporter with super-sleuthing skills, you probably wouldn't even notice. But ever since Michael told Hailey that the whole "Eeek, a mouse!" incident had been Greg's way of getting her attention, I could tell she was starting to see him in a different light. (Hailey is terrified of mice and bugs, and Greg teased her once in a movie theater, yelling "EEK!" and she was totally embarrassed. Michael told her it was because Greg actually kind of had a crush on her, which made Hailey feel a lot better.)

The crowd that had gathered around the battered remains of Mr. Cougar began to slowly drift off toward the field. The bleachers filled up pretty quickly, so I had to weigh my desire to stay and poke around the scene against the need to get a seat that would give me the best view of the star quarterback. Guess which way the scale tipped? Front-row-center bleacher seats, look out!

I grabbed Hailey's hand and scurried toward the field. On the way, I caught snippets of people's conversations. *Who do you think did it? I heard Danny Stratham from West Hills got suspended four times last year. I bet it was him. I'll never pass the earthonomics midterm without Mr. Cougar!* Good thing I always carried my reporter's notebook wherever I went. As soon as we sat down, I started jotting down notes. I stopped when the teams ran onto the field. Something wasn't right.

The Cherry Valley Cougars don't have the best record in the league, but they always play like they know they can win, even when they're facing a tough opponent like West Hills. Except that they didn't look confident—they looked concerned. I could tell by

looking at their faces that they had seen Mr. Cougar.
I wished I had been in the locker room to give them a
pregame speech. *Martone Pumps Up the Cougars
and They Steamroll Their Way to a Victory!*

The only thing worse than the look on the players' faces was the way they played the game. The
Cherry Valley Cougars made Hailey look like
Nostradamus. Doomed, indeed. Michael threw
seven interceptions, Connor Bourke missed three
field goals, and the West Hills' running back
ran through the holes in the Cougars' defense
like they were made of Swiss cheese. West Hills
scored a whopping seventy-three points to our six.
The Cougars looked like a team that would make
a "Not So Top Ten" list.

The usually boisterous crowd was so quiet that
if you talked in your normal voice, it sounded like
you were screaming. I found that out when I said,
"This is ugly," to Hailey, and everyone sitting on
the bleachers turned around and scowled at me.

"Guess Scoops is out of the question," Hailey
whispered.

"I'd say so," I agreed. "No one's going to want

to celebrate now." Especially, I thought, Michael. I felt bad for him. He looked frustrated, and I knew that he got really upset with himself when he felt he wasn't doing his best. I thought about describing the mood, since that's an exercise we did a lot in English class.

Somber. Dismal. Dejected. I have an app on my phone that helps me build vocabulary skills (because reporters *have* to be word masters), and these were a few of the words that I scribbled in my notebook before Hailey and I left the bleachers.

"Do you mind if we wait by the locker room?" I asked Hailey. "I just want to . . ."

Hailey finished my sentence for me. "See Michael Lawrence."

"Yeah, something like that." I smirked.

We hung around the locker room, trying to look nonchalant, cringing each time we heard the slam of one of the locker doors or the sound of a water bottle being thrown against the wall. The football team was obviously not a happy group. One by one, the players skulked out, their heads hanging down in defeat. I couldn't help but smile, though, when I saw a mop of dark hair heading my way.

"Good game," I lied. It was an incredibly dumb thing to say, but I couldn't help myself.

Michael Lawrence, losing Cougar quarterback and legendary dreamboat, rolled his bright blue eyes at me.

*Martone Fumbles with Cheesiest Cliché Ever.*

"I'm sorry," I said. "It's just one game. You'll get them next time."

I was really on a cliché roll now.

"I know you're trying to be nice," Michael said. "But please stop. It's not just one game. It's our luck. It's run out."

It was my turn to eye roll. And snort, although not intentionally.

"You're joking, right?" I asked.

"I'm not," Michael replied. "I don't know if we'll even win another game this season."

"You actually believe in the Mr. Cougar superstition?" I said, shocked. "Do you believe in the tooth fairy and the Easter Bunny, too?"

Michael didn't answer either question. He just stormed off without saying a word.

Hailey looked at me sympathetically. It was not the kind of look you want your best friend to give you right after you were talking to the love of your life and had maybe just blown it. *It had I wish I could give you a do-over; you messed that one up so royally* written all over it.

"I know, okay, so please don't say anything," I said to Hailey. "I was just hoping he could put aside his football helmet and think about it from a reporter's perspective. But I guess it's too soon."

"Speaking of reporters," Hailey said, "check it out."

Hailey pointed to a WKDH news van that was parked across the street from the school. I had to blink my eyes to make sure I wasn't hallucinating. It certainly took my mind off of my disastrous Michael Lawrence encounter. April Weathers, award-winning television journalist, was exiting the van. A camera operator followed behind her.

"O. . . M . . . ," I shouted.

"G!" Hailey finished my exclamation for me.

"IT'S APRIL WEATHERS!"

"No," I corrected. "It's April 'Peabody-Award-Winning' Weathers. And she's heading our way!"

What happened next seemed like a dream sequence. April Weathers, one of my journalistic idols, actually opened her mouth and spoke to me.

"Excuse me, ladies," she said in a voice that sounded as if she had perfected her reporter's tone with years of practice. "Would you mind if I asked you a few questions?"

"M-m-mind?" I stammered. "Not at all." The cameraman turned on the light and it was really bright and hot. I suddenly realized I could end up on the evening news, and I got a little nervous.

"How do you feel about what happened to the statue of Cherry Valley's mascot?" April Weathers asked.

"I think it's terrible," I said. "I don't know why anyone would want to do that to a harmless piece of stone."

"I agree," Hailey added. "No one messes with Mr. Cougar and gets away with it. It's just wrong."

"Do you think that whoever did this wanted to

bring bad luck to Cherry Valley?" questioned April.

"I do!" Hailey said. "Everyone knows it's good luck to rub Mr. Cougar's paw. That's why whoever did this destroyed the paw!"

"Well, if that was their motive, it was a pretty silly one." I chuckled. "If you believe in facts, like I do, you know that there's no such thing as good, or bad, luck. Right, April?"

April Weathers smiled at me, winked, then reached into her pocket and pulled out a set of keys. At the end of the key chain was a furry pink rabbit's foot. Ugh! First I blow it with Michael Lawrence and now with April Weathers. Maybe there was something to this Mr. Cougar thing.

"Do you have any idea who might have done it?" April asked.

I pulled out my reporter's notebook, trying to impress her. "Well, I've been keeping track of what people have been saying," I said, "and it seems like almost everyone thinks that it was someone from West Hills. And for the record, at least one person mentioned the name 'Danny Stratham.'"

"Cut!" April Weathers said as she turned to the

camera operator. "Roll back and edit that out."

Then she put her arm around me. "I can see that you have an interest in reporting," she said.

"I do!" I said proudly. "I'm a reporter for the *Cherry Valley Voice*."

She smiled again. "Here's a tip. Repeating gossip or something that's hearsay, or what you've heard people saying, isn't something you can report. It's called speculation. A lot of the time it turns out that person wasn't involved, but if you name them, it can be very harmful and hurtful, especially if it's connected to a crime. That's why we're really careful about these things. This may look like some kind of a prank gone wrong, but it's vandalism, and that's a crime."

"I'm so sorry," I said, feeling as dejected as the Cougar players. I also felt really stupid. I should have known that. I do know that! We learned it in Journalism 101, for goodness' sake! I'd just gotten so excited and, well, I had wanted to impress April.

"Oh, don't be sorry. I just wanted to steer you in the right direction for the future," she said cheerfully. "I can tell you're serious about reporting. I was too, when I was your age. And I have some news for you. You're going to be on television tonight. Make sure to watch WKDH news at six p.m."

"WE WILL!" Hailey and I screamed at the same time.

We didn't want to look immature in front of an award-winning journalist, so we waited until April Weathers had walked out of sight, and then we grabbed each other and started jumping up and down. Hailey's dad walked over and looked at us, perplexed.

"I thought we lost the game," he said.

"We did, Dad!" Hailey said. "But we're going to be on the news tonight!"

"And April Weathers said I'm just like her!" I shouted.

"Not exactly." Hailey laughed. "But close enough."

"Oh, okay." Hailey's dad laughed too. "In that case, let's get you home so you can set your DVR!"

# Chapter 3

## CURSE HITS HARD; CHERRY VALLEY PANICS

★ ★ ★

The next morning the school was buzzing with excitement. Everyone was talking about what happened to Mr. Cougar and *everyone* thought that a West Hills student was responsible. The name of the day seemed to be Danny Stratham, even though I now knew better than to report that name until I gathered some hard evidence that proved he was involved. Thanks, April Weathers!

Too bad April hadn't gotten to the rest of the school. The stories about Danny Stratham were becoming wilder by the minute.

"Did you hear that Danny Stratham has to report to the dean's office every afternoon because he's in trouble all the time?" Hailey asked as she breezed over to my locker.

"No," I replied. "Where did you hear that?"

"Jeff Perry said that he knows a kid who knows a kid who's Danny Stratham's cousin," Hailey answered.

"That's a real reliable source." I laughed. "And shouldn't the vice president of Cherry Valley Middle School be a little more considerate about spreading rumors?"

Hailey's cheeks turned red. She takes her responsibilities as student body vice president very seriously.

"You're right," she said. "It's just that everyone's talking about him."

"Talking about who?" Jenna asked, as she and Kristen squeezed in between Hailey and me as we walked down the hall to our first class.

"Danny Stratham," Hailey said.

"Oh, yeah, he's bad news," Jenna said. "I heard he once kicked a neighbor's dog on the way to school just to show off how mean he is."

"Jenna!" I said, alarmed. "That's ridiculous."

"No, it's true. I heard that, too!" said Kristen.

"Everyone knows he's the one who vandalized Mr. Cougar."

"Everyone *thinks* that," I corrected her. "But no one knows, because there's no proof."

"We'll see," Jenna replied. "Did you see the way he was laughing and smiling at the end of the game? He looked pretty guilty to me."

"Um, maybe he was laughing and smiling because his team had just won by almost seventy points?" I asked. "And he set a West Hills record with eight touchdown receptions?"

"Maybe," said Jenna. "We'll see."

Then she dropped her voice to a whisper. "I heard he wanted to get a tattoo when he was six years old, but his mother wouldn't let him," she said.

"That's enough!" I said. "No more Danny Stratham talk!"

"Okay, fine," huffed Kristen. "What, do you have a crush on him or something? We all know how much you like football players. Does Samantha Martone only like winners?"

Kristen, Jenna, and even Hailey laughed. I

stormed off to Spanish class.

There was definitely a disturbance in the Cherry Valley force. Mrs. Cassas said, "*Class, bonne journée,*" which is French, at the beginning of *Spanish* class and then she took out a French textbook! A frog escaped in the science lab and caused eleven minutes of chaos until John Scott heroically captured it in a beaker. Missy Davis slipped on some pudding in the cafeteria and went flying through the air in a fall that was worthy of a blooper reel.

"Bad luck reigns at Cherry Valley," Hailey noted, scooping white rice with salt and butter into her mouth, her typical lunch. "Told ya."

"Whatever," I said. "The only bad luck I'm having is that I haven't seen Michael all day. I wonder if he's avoiding me."

"Hmmm," Hailey said. "Now that I think about it, I haven't seen him either. He's probably just lying low and feeling sorry for himself. It was a bad loss yesterday, especially if you're the quarterback."

"It was," I agreed. "I guess I'll find out later at our newspaper meeting."

If you are a fan of the strong, silent type, you would have fallen head over heels in love with the Michael Lawrence who attended the newspaper meeting later that afternoon. Michael almost always had strong opinions to share, but I guess he decided to keep them to himself. He wasn't sitting by my side in our usual spot on the love seat, either (yes, there's a love seat in the office, and I *love* sitting in it with Michael Lawrence). He was slouched in a chair on the other side of the room. Maybe he was going for the sullen loser look. I think I heard Allie say that was popular on the fashion runways this year.

Mr. Trigg, on the other hand, was a whirlwind of excitement.

"Ladies and Gentlemen!" he announced as he gathered the *Cherry Valley Voice* team together in the newsroom. "We've had quite the incident! And it is our job as journalists to investigate and report what we've found to our peers!

"Samantha Martone, I spied your familiar face on my television screen last evening," he continued.

"Nice quote. You and Mr. Lawrence also did a stellar job on the school election pieces, so I'd like you to continue that tradition with an investigation into the cougar statue story. Good luck."

"More like bad luck," grumbled Michael.

"What was that, Mr. Lawrence?" Trigg asked. "Did you have something to add to the conversation?"

"No. I'll work on the story with Sam," said Michael. "I'm just not hopeful that we'll be able to dig up any answers."

"Mr. Lawrence," Trigg replied. "Winston Churchill once said, 'The pessimist sees difficulty in every opportunity. The optimist sees the opportunity in every difficulty.' I highly encourage you to channel your optimistic side for this assignment."

"Got it," Michael said as he slumped back into his seat.

Normally, I would have taken his behavior personally, considering our failed conversation outside the locker room, but I was too excited by the thought of reporting an actual news story to get upset by it. Any other day, Michael's behavior would have sent me into a panic, but now I was actually getting a little ticked off. He needed to stop pouting like a baby and get to work.

As Mr. Trigg handed out the assignments for the rest of the team, I tried to look casual and cool as I sauntered over to Michael's chair.

"Hey, Michael, this is going to be great, right?" I said. "We get to investigate a real crime!"

I was almost positive that I had spoken loud enough for Michael to hear me, but he didn't respond.

"Earth to Michael," I said even louder. "Do you read me?"

"Huh?" Michael said as he looked up at me, distracted by his own gloomy thoughts. "Oh, Sam. Hey, what's up?"

"Did you hear Mr. Trigg?" I asked. "We're working together on the cougar story. It's only the biggest news story Cherry Valley Middle School has ever had."

"Yeah, I heard him," Michael said. "It's big news, all right. Everyone is talking about it. I can't wait to find out who did this. The whole football team can't wait to find out who did this."

"Okay," I said, trying to stay calm. "Let's focus on our job as *Cherry Valley Voice* reporters, shall we?" I continued, trying to sound detached and professional.

"Sure," said Michael. "What's your plan?"

"Well, first, I think we need to get some advice from Mr. Trigg," I told him. "This is real news, and we haven't worked on anything this big before."

"Okay, that sounds reasonable," Michael agreed.

It could have been my imagination, but I had a feeling that the sullen football Michael was being pushed aside by the excited reporter Michael a teensy little bit.

Mr. Trigg relished his role as advisor to the news team. He was thrilled to sit with Michael and me after the meeting to go over proper procedure and give us some tips for getting started. In fact, he had already done some of the work for us. He gave us the name of the police officer who was leading the investigation and said that most reporters begin with the official side of the story by getting a copy of the police report and talking to the officers who collected evidence from the crime scene.

"We need to e-mail Officer Mendez and schedule a time to meet her," I said.

"Would you mind doing that?" Michael asked. "I'm meeting with Coach Dixon after this to go over our plan for the game against Valley View. If we have another loss like the one to West Hills, we could get knocked out of the playoffs."

"Sure, no problem," I replied. "I'll do it as soon as I get home."

"And, Michael . . . ," I added, a bit nervously, "I'm sorry if I seemed insensitive after the game. I know it was a tough loss."

"It was," Michael admitted. "I was awful."

"It wasn't just you," I said. "The rest of the team was terrible too."

"I'll tell the guys you said that, Pasty." He chuckled.

Great. *Martone Insults Entire Cougar Football Team, Including the Love of Her Life; Gets Banned from Future Games.*

★  ★  ★

Later that night, I asked my mom to read over my e-mail to Officer Mendez. Even though I'm confident in my writing skills, I had to admit I was a little nervous about contacting a police officer. Mom proofread it and showed me how to rephrase some of my sentences to make them sound more professional.

"This is really great, Sam. I'm so proud of you," she said when I hit send. "Am I still allowed to say that, or is that too embarrassing?"

"You can still say that." I laughed. "I'm actually proud of myself. I can't wait to dig deeper into this story and find out what really happened."

"Okay, just remember, it was a crime," said Mom. "And even though no one was hurt, there can be danger involved. So keep Mr. Trigg and me informed about everything you do, and be smart."

"That's impossible," Allie snarked as she walked past Mom's office. "I got all the smart genes. You just got lucky. And speaking of luck," she added, "I heard the black cloud of bad luck has already parked itself over Cherry Valley Middle School. Is that true?"

"Come on, Allie. Be real," I said. "Every little thing looks like bad luck now. That's what everyone's focused on. There's no such thing."

★   ★   ★

The rest of the week appeared to be some kind of cosmic sign intended to prove me wrong. Murphy's Law was in full effect: *Anything that can go wrong, will go wrong.*

On Tuesday, I walked into school to find Hailey on her hands and knees, crawling around the lockers.

"Is this some kind of strange soccer drill?" I asked.

"Weird," Hailey replied. "I lost my new sunglasses, and I can't find them anywhere. I thought I put them in my locker, but maybe I dropped them."

Just then, Anthony Wright came running over to talk to Hailey. Before he could say a word, we heard a crunching sound. Hailey put her head in her hands and moaned.

"Thanks, Anthony," I said. "You just found Hailey's sunglasses."

"And you don't believe in the Cougar Curse,"

Hailey sighed, holding her broken sunglasses.

On Wednesday, I saw Jenna sitting in the lunchroom by herself, crying. Hailey and I went to sit with her and found out that she had failed the math test.

"I studied for two weeks!" Jenna said. "And math is my best subject. This has to be because of the curse."

"Sure seems that way," Hailey said as she glared in my direction.

On Thursday, Hailey and I went to watch Anthony Wright compete against West Hills in a chess competition after school. He went to make a move during the match and knocked the whole board onto the floor. It was the first time that had ever happened to him, and he's been playing chess since he was three!

"Cougar Curse," Hailey whispered to me. "Just sayin'."

Friday was the worst day of the week, though. The Cherry Valley Cougars were facing the Valley View Vipers. The Vipers had a one-and-eight record, and if you had asked anyone before the cougar incident to predict the game outcome, even a Viper fan, they would have said the Cougars would win in a blowout. I knew the game wasn't going to go well even before it started. Michael Lawrence and the other players on the team looked like they had been invaded by body snatchers.

Usually on game day, the guys on the team give each other high fives every time they pass in the hallway. They growl, "Cougars, yeah!" so much, it made you wonder if they knew how to say anything else.

Before Friday's game, all signs of team spirit had been erased. Michael and his teammates might have been playing for Anthony's chess team. I didn't see a single high five, or hear any "Cougars, yeah!" chants. So yeah, I knew the game was not going to be a good one.

I just didn't know how bad it would be. It was one thing to fumble the ball five times, but when Connor Bourke fell to the ground and clutched his ankle in pain, even I groaned. He was the only kicker on the team who could even reach the goal posts. Without Connor, the Cougars really did look doomed.

Oh yeah, and they lost the game, too. It wasn't a romp like the game against West Hills. It came down to the last play of the game, and that's when Brandon Abrenica intercepted the ball and ran it in for Valley View's winning touchdown. Final score: twenty-six to twenty-one. Ouch!

I didn't bother waiting for Michael after the game. I knew what his reaction would be, and anyway, I had investigating to do. Everyone else in Cherry Valley could walk on eggshells because of the Cougar Curse. It wasn't going to stop Samantha Martone, girl reporter extraordinaire, from doing her job.

# Chapter 4

## ALL WORK AND NO PLAY MAKES MARTONE A GREAT REPORTER

★ ★ ★

Back at home, Allie and her friends had completely taken over the kitchen. Mural paper stretched from the refrigerator to the kitchen door, and Allie looked like she had taken a bath in glitter glue.

"School project?" I asked. "On a Friday night?"

"Yup," said Ashley Flynn. "We have to depict a historical event we've learned about this semester in an inventive way. It's due on Monday. We decided to combine it with a sleepover."

"And this event is . . . ?" I wondered as I looked at globs of glue on the mural paper.

"The Battle of Gettysburg, duh," Allie huffed.

"Wow! Combining war and glitter glue is definitely an original concept," I noted.

"Hey, Sam, how's that Cougar Curse going?" Ashley Diaz chimed in.

"Oh, I don't believe in the curse," I answered. "But what's really exciting is that I'm investigating the story for the school paper. I'm going to interview police involved, get information from the first people to arrive at the scene, and talk to students at Cherry Valley *and* West Hills—"

"Um, Sam," Allie interrupted. "*My* friends. *Your* room."

Allie pointed her finger toward my room as if she were ordering me to leave her presence. While I walked away, I could hear Allie and the Ashleys burst into a fit of giggles. Sometimes Allie could be kind of cool, but most of the time, she's, well . . . a big sister. Ugh!

I kicked off my sneakers and turned on my computer. Some people might get distracted and waste their time poking around on Buddybook or making a wish list on their favorite shopping site. I was focused on the investigation. I checked my e-mail and saw that Officer Mendez had replied.

Dear Miss Martone,

I received your e-mail request. I'd be happy to talk to you and Mr. Lawrence about the case. We can arrange a meeting at the precinct one afternoon next week. Let me know what day and time work best for you. We will need to keep the meeting under thirty minutes, so please prepare your questions in advance.

Looking forward to meeting you.

Sincerely,

Officer Jeanine Mendez

Perfect! I was tempted to write back right away and suggest the best day and time to meet, but I knew that wouldn't be fair to Michael. Now I had a dilemma. Should I put my eagerness on the backburner and wait to call Michael tomorrow, or should I keep things moving forward and call him on a Friday night, after another heartbreaking Cougar loss? If Allie hadn't been so rude, I would have asked for her advice, but from the sound of the shrieks coming from the kitchen, I knew I was on my own. I had so much nervous energy, I decided to channel it into making a pros vs. cons chart.

|  | PROS | CONS |
|---|---|---|
| CALL NOW | • keep the investigation moving forward<br><br>• channel my nervous energy<br><br>• get to talk to Michael Lawrence | • Michael might not be in the mood to talk after the football game<br><br>• Officer Mendez probably isn't going to read her e-mail on a Friday night anyway<br><br>• Michael might not be home and I might have to talk to one of his brothers |
| CALL TOMORROW | • give Michael time to sleep on the loss<br><br>• have time to work on my e-mail reply to Officer Mendez | • I WON'T BE ABLE TO SLEEP!!!! |

I sat on my bed, staring at the chart, still unable to make a decision. And then I did something that I wasn't sure was the best use of my reporter skills, but that had been itching my brain for the past few days. I typed "Danny Stratham" and "West Hills" into a search engine. I looked at my computer screen for what seemed like an eternity, but was probably no more than fifteen seconds, and then I hit the return key.

There weren't a lot of entries, only ten, in fact. None of them referred to suspensions or a criminal record, dog-kicking or tattoos. Eight were about West Hills football games and his role as a star receiver. One was about a volunteer park cleanup that he'd helped to organize. The last showed a picture of him and the West Hills principal—Patricia Stratham, his mom!

I printed it out because I couldn't wait to show to Jenna, Kristen, and Hailey the real reason that Danny Stratham went to the principal's office every afternoon. I looked at my chart again and then my clock and decided that even if it meant a sleepless night, it would probably be best to wait until tomorrow to call Michael. I decided to forward Officer Mendez's e-mail to him instead with a quick note. Except that my "quick" note took about twenty minutes to write, because I kept rewriting the first line.

Hey, Michael,

~~Sorry about the loss to Valley View.~~

~~That was a tough game.~~

~~You played a lot better than you did in the game against West Hills.~~

It seemed impossible to get the "friendly, encouraging, and concerned" tone I wanted, so I decided to just stick to the facts.

Hey, Michael,

See below. Officer Mendez will meet with us. What day/time is best for you?

—Sam

I almost fell out of bed when my computer chimed a minute later. Michael had already e-mailed me back! It said only:

Want to talk?

So I replied:

Sure. Call me whenever you want. I'm home.

The phone rang almost immediately. Michael obviously was in need of a diversion from thinking about football.

"I GOT IT! I GOT IT I GOT IT!" I yelled out my bedroom door as I grabbed the phone.

"Hi, Michael," I heard Allie say with a giggle. "Sam's here. Hold on a minute."

"Hi, Michael," I said on the other receiver. "I got it, Allie. You can hang up now."

I heard a *click*, and then it sounded like a herd of cattle were thumping down the hall outside my room. Allie, Ashley, and Ashley poked their heads into my bedroom.

"Are his brothers home?" Ashley Diaz whispered.

"Could you ask?" Allie said.

"Um, Allie," I replied, covering the receiver.

"*My* call. *Your* room." I pointed to her room across the hall. Payback is awesome!

"Sorry about that, Michael," I said into the phone. "Allie and her friends are having a sleepover and they're driving me a little nuts."

"No problem," Michael replied. "I have brothers. I know the feeling.

"Oh, and before you say anything," he added, "can we *not* talk about football?"

"Football? What's that?" I joked.

"Exactly," Michael said. "Thank you."

I filled Michael in on the details, including my "background check" on Danny Stratham. I was surprised when Michael started to laugh.

"Danny Stratham? Really, Sam?" He chuckled. "He's only one of the nicest guys on the West Hills team. He always shows great sportsmanship. I would never suspect that he would do it."

"Well, you and I may be the only Cherry Valley students who think that," I said, a little miffed. "His name was spreading through the school like the flu virus in February."

"That's just because he looks tough," Michael

said. "I think we can safely cross him off the suspect list. I'll vouch for him."

"Okay, I'll take your word for it," I replied.
"Speaking of suspects, is there anyone on your
list? Anyone from West Hills?"

"From West Hills?" asked Michael. "No, I
can't think of anyone. They're all pretty nice guys,
even though they're the enemy."

"Right, but the playoffs are coming up," I
reminded Michael. "Everyone said that Cherry
Valley is the only team that can take the championship away from West Hills. Even nice guys
will sometimes do questionable things to get a
competitive edge."

"No way!" Michael protested. "They wouldn't
do that."

It seemed a little strange to me that Michael
would defend West Hills, but maybe it was some
sort of football brotherhood thing that I didn't
know about.

"Fine. We said we weren't going to talk about
football anyway," I reminded him. "Let's just figure out when we can meet with Officer Mendez."

Michael and I came up with a few suggestions, and I wrote our reply to Officer Mendez and sent it.

I knew I always fumbled when I talked to Michael about football, but I also knew that he was feeling down and I wanted to make him feel better.

"Michael, I'm really glad Mr. Trigg gave us this story," I said. "I think we can really do some great work here . . . maybe even break the case and find out who did it!"

The line was silent for a few seconds.

"Michael? Are you still there?" I asked.

"Oh, yeah, sorry, I'm here," Michael replied. "Sam . . . ?"

Michael's voice trailed off. I could hear sadness in it, and I wished I could make it go away. These games must have really gotten to him.

"Yes, Michael," I answered.

"Good night," he said abruptly. "Have a great weekend."

After I hung up, I looked at the phone in disbelief. Michael Lawrence definitely hadn't just been going to say good night, so what *had* he been going to say before he stopped himself?

I heard screams coming from Allie's room and knew that the scary moviefest had begun. I flopped down onto my bed, grabbed my pillow, and put it over my face. Samantha Martone, meet sleepless night.

# Chapter 5

## MARTONE MEETS IDOL, LOSES ABILITY TO SPEAK

★ ★ ★

Tuesday afternoon, Michael Lawrence and I headed to the Cherry Valley Police Station. We had hardly spoken at all since the phone call on Friday night, so while his mom drove, we used the time in the car to go over our plans.

"Here's my list of questions," I said, taking out my notebook and showing it to Michael. "What do you think?"

Michael's mom passed back a plastic bag filled with freshly baked oatmeal-raisin cookies.

"I figured you guys might need an after-school energy boost," she said.

"Thanks, Mrs. Lawrence," I said as I popped a cookie into my mouth. "These are delicious. I can see where Michael gets his baking skills."

Michael handed me another cookie and then pointed to my notebook.

"Looks good, Snacky," he said. "I think you've got it covered."

Michael always makes up nicknames for me to tease me. Hopefully he was in a better mood today if he was joking around.

"We only have a half hour," I said. "I don't want to take time away from your questions. Do you have a list we can go over so we don't repeat anything?"

Michael tapped his temple, obviously referring to his ridiculously reliable memory. "My list of questions is right here, Martone," he said. "And don't worry. I won't repeat any of your questions. I think it's better if you take the lead on this one anyway."

"Okay, if you're sure," I said. "Let's do this!"

We headed into the police station. I was so excited and nervous, I felt like a swarm of caterpillars had cocooned in my stomach and were now emerging as butterflies. I tried to hide it and look professional. I had never been in a police station before, and it was a teeny tiny bit scary.

"Are you okay?" Michael asked.

"Yeah, why?" I answered.

"I don't know. You look a little stone-faced," he said.

Thank you, Michael Lawrence, for your honest assessment. Stone-faced was definitely not the look I was going for, so I took a deep breath and tried to relax. It was a challenge, because the frenzy of activity inside the police station was somewhat overwhelming, and I could tell the place was just *filled* with news stories. Just then, a tall woman wearing a dark blue uniform approached us.

"Samantha Martone?" she asked.

"Yes," I replied, and I held out my hand when I saw her name tag. "Nice to meet you, Officer Mendez. This is my partner on the story, Michael Lawrence."

Officer Mendez shook my hand firmly, then turned to Michael. It was hard not to stare at the gun holster strapped around her waist, but I tried my best.

"Let's go somewhere we can talk privately," she said.

We followed Officer Mendez through a maze of cubbies; then she led us into an interrogation room. "This is where we interview our subjects," she said. "It's a different process from your investigation, but not so different."

Michael and I sat across the table from Officer Mendez. I took out a small recording device from my bag. Mr. Trigg had told us that since this was an official investigation, it would be best to document our interviews with something more than my notes or Michael's photographic memory.

"Do you mind if I record the interview?" I asked Officer Mendez. "Just to make sure that we accurately represent anything you say."

"I don't mind at all," she replied. "I'd actually insist on doing it myself, if you didn't ask. It's for both of our protection.

"Also," she continued, "I'll need to see a copy of your story before it's printed. I have to make sure it won't interfere with the investigation or misrepresent the facts. I hope you understand."

"I do," I said. "I hope you understand that I'll have to check with our advisor, Mr. Trigg, before I can agree to that. But I'm sure it won't be a problem."

Michael kicked my foot under the table, as if to say, *Way to be professional, Martone!*

"Sure. You can let me know by e-mail," Officer Mendez replied. "If I don't hear from you, I'll contact your advisor directly. Now, let's get the tape rolling. We don't have a lot of time." Boy, she was all business.

I pressed the record button and did a quick test, just to make sure that we could hear everyone in the room clearly—another Mr. Trigg tip. Then I turned to my list of questions.

"Officer Mendez, can you tell us how the police were first alerted to the cougar incident and what they saw when they arrived on the scene?"

"There was an anonymous 911 call that alerted us to the incident," Officer Mendez began. "We sent two officers in a patrol car to the crime scene. They cordoned off the area and called in the investigative unit. They looked for any signs of evidence and dusted for fingerprints."

"About what time did the police arrive?" I asked.

"The patrol car arrived on the scene at ten

forty-five a.m.," Officer Mendez reported. "The investigative team arrived at eleven eighteen a.m. All well before the crowd started gathering for the game."

I noticed that Michael's leg was shaking up and down. I had no idea what that was about. Maybe he was as nervous about doing an official interview as I was.

"Did they find any evidence?" Michael asked.

"Nothing that's been useful yet," answered Officer Mendez. "They found fingerprints on the statue, especially on the area around the broken paw, but there's no way to know if they belong to students or to the perpetrators."

"Perpetrators?" Michael asked. "It's a broken statue."

"It's a crime," Officer Mendez said. "We take vandalism seriously. If we identify the perpetrators and the school decides to press charges, then the consequences for those individuals could be severe."

"Like jail time?" Michael asked.

I could swear that I actually saw him gulp after

he asked that question. He looked a little pale, too.

"Probably not jail time, no, unless they have a prior record," Officer Mendez admitted. "But it could go on their permanent record, and they may be served with a community service sentence. It's hard to say, because it depends on the justice system. We just apprehend the perpetrators. We don't decide what happens to them."

"Do you have any suspects?" I asked.

"We don't have any particular suspects at the moment," Officer Mendez said. "And if we did, I wouldn't be able share their names with you. Let's just say that the Cherry Valley police force considers the vandalism that occurred at Cherry Valley Middle School to be a serious offense, and we will continue our investigation until we are able to locate the person or persons who are responsible for it."

Michael and I continued to ask questions about the incident. I don't know that we learned a lot more than we already knew, but it was still worthwhile to get some official quotes to add to our story and to get the experience of interviewing a police officer. When exactly thirty minutes had passed, Officer Mendez pushed back her chair and said it was time to wrap up.

"Thank you so much," I said as I shook her hand good-bye. "I'll make sure to let you know what Mr. Trigg says."

"Yes, thank you," Michael added. "We know your time is valuable, and we really appreciate that you took the time to talk to us."

Before Officer Mendez could respond, we heard someone shouting her name. A woman wearing charcoal-gray slacks and a white Oxford shirt came rushing over.

"Hey, Mendez, I'm on deadline," she panted. "Got anything new for me?"

Officer Mendez smiled at us. "Just finishing up here," she said. "Samantha and Michael, meet Lauren Fields, reporter for the *Cherry Valley Gazette*."

*Lauren Fields!* This was incredible. I read her stories in the newspaper every day. What were the odds that I would meet two of my journalism idols before I even graduated middle school? I grinned like the Cheshire cat. I had so much I wanted to say, but the words weren't forming in my mouth.

"Nice to meet you, Ms. Fields," Michael said. "This is my writing partner, Samantha Martone. We're working on a story for our school newspaper."

"The *Cherry Valley Voice*!" Ms. Fields cried. "I know you two. I read your stories."

"You do?" I asked, dumbfounded.

"I really do," she replied. "It's a great way for me to see what issues are hitting home in Cherry Valley, especially with the younger audience. The article you wrote about pay to play was really well done. Bravo!"

"We're reporting on the cougar incident," Michael explained. "Do you have leads on that story?"

Impressive work, Michael Lawrence. Photographic memory *and* the ability to think on your feet. No wonder I like you so much.

"Nope, none yet," Ms. Fields confessed. "That's why I'm here, working the police beat. You guys probably know more than I do at this point."

She squinted her eyes, leaned toward Michael,

and stared right into his baby blues. "Do you?" she asked.

I needed to remember that trick the next time I was interviewing someone. Michael looked like he had been totally thrown off guard. And he didn't even know anything more than I did!

Lauren Fields started laughing and slapped Michael on the back.

"I'm sorry," she said. "I'm just kidding. I'm actually taking the angle that the whole school rivalry thing is getting out of hand. The tension between these schools and their sports teams is insane—and totally inappropriate for your age group, by the way."

I took out my notebook and scribbled some thoughts. That was an interesting way of looking at the story, and I'd never even considered it.

"Here's my card," Ms. Fields said as she handed Michael and me each a business card. "If you hear anything interesting, shoot me an e-mail or give me a call. And if you ever want a tour of the newsroom, we can probably arrange that, too."

"Are you serious?" I gasped. "That would be

incredible. Thank you so much!"

"Okay, we'll figure something out another time," she said. "Like I said when I first got here, I'm on a deadline, so I'm going to talk to Officer Mendez and let you two get back to your reporting."

Somehow Michael and I left the police station, got back into his mother's car, drove all the way to my house, and said good-bye to each other, but if you asked me exactly what happened, I wouldn't be able to tell you. I think I spent the whole time staring at Lauren Fields's business card and imagining what it would be like if my name were on the card instead of hers.

★     ★     ★

On Wednesday, Michael and I told Mr. Trigg about our meeting with Officer Mendez. He took it as an opportunity to give us a Journalism 101 refresher course.

"I don't think Officer Mendez's request is unreasonable, considering this is a school newspaper," he told us. "So you can e-mail her and tell her that you will send her the story when it's finished. But I do need you to know that it is not a practice you have to continue as a professional journalist. You're under no obligation to get approval from the people you quote, even from officials like a police officer, if you quote them accurately and keep a record from the interview, like the recording you made. This way, if anyone ever accuses you of representing them inaccurately, you can show them the proof behind your words."

I scribbled frantically in my notebook as Mr. Trigg spoke. I could listen to him talk about journalism all day, and it wasn't just because of the dignified British accent. Everyone has a passion, and you can tell what that passion is because when you're in the middle of it, you don't care what else is happening around you. That's how I feel about the news.

"Sam, we should probably figure out our next steps," Michael said wisely.

Have I mentioned how much I love the way his brain works?

"Right," I agreed. "What are you thinking?"

"I think we should talk to some of the kids at West Hills," Michael said. "I can start with the guys I know on the team and then branch out from there. I have some ideas about who might be involved, so I'm going to try to feel them out."

"Oh really?" I asked. "You know as journalists we have to remain neutral and fair in our reporting. Do you think you can be that way toward your football nemeses?

"I was thinking we might explore the Cougar Curse angle a little more," I added. "Maybe we can start there."

"Perfect, Pasty!" Michael replied. "You can take West Hills, since I'm 'biased,' and I'll talk to some Cherry Valley kids about the curse."

Somehow, this conversation hadn't gone the way I'd thought it would, but I didn't see a way that I could back out now. Michael's plan made sense, but it meant that I would have to go it alone when I would have much rather spent the time with my favorite baby-blue-eyed partner. Maybe the Cougar Curse was trying to tell me something.

# Chapter 6

## WEST HILLS' LADIES' MAN MAKES A MOVE

★ ★ ★

Michael Lawrence may have been friendly with the guys on the West Hills football team, but I had my own West Hills connections. My mom's best friend, April, lives in West Hills. They've known each other since kindergarten, and April's known me since before I was born. She has a daughter, Emma, who's just a year younger than I am. Of course, Mom and April had dreamed that Emma and I would be BFFs, just like they are, but that didn't exactly pan out.

Don't get me wrong. I like Emma, and whenever we all get together, we have fun hanging out. It's just that she's very . . . West Hills. Again, I don't mean that in a bad way. It's just that Emma and her friends are into different kinds of things than my friends and I are into.

Like horses . . . and saddles . . . and riding competitions . . . and riding outfits . . . and, well, you get my point.

Anyway, I really do like Emma, and she was my best chance of getting a West Hills source, so when I got home from school I sent her an e-mail asking what the kids at West Hills were saying about the cougar incident. I had a pile of homework to do, so I shut off the computer and opened my math book. Twelve math word problems, two short responses about mechanical and chemical weathering, a review of my Spanish flash cards, and an hour of reading my book club book later, I was ready to get back to Mr. Cougar—after a snack, of course.

Emma had sent me a reply:

Hi, Sam,

I wish Cherry Valley would just drop the whole cougar thing. It's crazy. Everyone just assumed someone from our school did it because we're rivals. Where's your proof?

This is giving our school a bad reputation. I hope you'll
include our side in your story.

I talked to some of my friends, and they agreed to talk
to you. I'll text you their info. They're all home right
now, so it would be good to call soon.

—Emma

Emma's reply made me really happy that I had
gotten my homework out of the way. I called Evie
Fong first, since I had met her with Emma once
before.

"Hi, Evie. This is Samantha Martone," I
greeted her. "I think Emma told you I'd be calling
about a story I'm working on."

"Hi, Sam. What's going on?" replied Evie.
"Emma said she told you how upset everyone is
at West Hills."

"She did," I said. "What's your take on it?"

"I think you guys at Cherry Valley are taking your cougar a little too seriously," Evie
answered. "I mean, believing in a curse—are
you joking? I thought that went out in the

Middle Ages or something."

"Oh, I totally agree with you there," I said. "I don't believe in curses either. But Mr. Cougar was a symbol of our school, and school property, so it's still not right that somebody vandalized the statue. Do you think someone at West Hills would have a grudge against us for some reason?"

"No one I know of," Evie replied. "Why would we have a grudge? We beat your football team in the last six championship games. It seems like the grudge would be the other way around."

"I didn't think of it that way," I admitted. "I just thought of the rivalry."

"I'd be shocked to find out that someone from West Hills did this," Evie said. "Honestly, I don't know anyone who would risk getting in that much trouble for something dumb like that."

"Thanks for talking to me, Evie," I said. "I'll definitely make sure West Hills's voice is heard in my story."

I called three other kids on Emma's list, and each one had a similar stance on the matter. *No, I don't know anyone at West Hills who would vandalize Mr. Cougar. Yes, I think the Cougar Curse is silly. Please let everyone know that West Hills had nothing to do with it.*

When I got to the last name on the list, I actually gasped. *Danny Stratham!* I hadn't known Emma was friends with him. Now, this was going to be interesting.

I dialed his number and held my breath. It sounded like an older man answered the phone— I guessed it was his dad.

"Hello, this is Samantha Martone. May I please speak to Danny?" I said in my most formal voice.

*"Danny!"* the man yelled. "There's another girl on the phone for you!"

Interesting. I guess Danny Stratham was a ladies' man. I hadn't known that about him either.

"Hello?" said a voice that sounded the way I would imagine Danny Stratham's voice to sound.

"Danny? This is Samantha Martone, Emma's friend," I explained.

"Oh, hey, Samantha," he said in a really friendly voice. "I think I've seen you around before at the football games. Emma described what you look like. I definitely remembered seeing you in the stands."

"You may have," I told him. "I'm at every game."

"Because you're Michael Lawrence's girlfriend, right?" he said.

"G-g-girlfriend?" I stammered. "No, we're, um, just friends. And writing partners. We're working on a story together right now about the cougar incident."

"Interesting," Danny replied.

"Oh, do you know something about what happened to Mr. Cougar?" I asked.

"No, I meant interesting that you're not Michael Lawrence's girlfriend," he said.

I could feel the blood rushing to my cheeks, and I was relieved that I had called Danny over the phone and not through a video chat. Was Danny Stratham actually flirting with me? Was I blushing because of it?

"I don't know if that's interesting or not. It's just a fact," I said. "I do know that I have a story to write about what happened to Cherry Valley's cougar statue. That's why I was calling."

"Yeah, that's what Emma told me," Danny said. "But I don't really know anything about that. I just thought it would be fun to talk to you."

"Really? I have to tell you, Danny, your name was mentioned all over Cherry Valley Middle School as someone who might be responsible," I informed him. "Not that I believed it, but that's what everyone else was saying."

"They're just jealous because I owned them on the football field that day." Danny laughed. "I'm working on getting a scholarship to college. Why would I mess with my future by breaking your dumb cougar?"

"I don't know," I said honestly. "Like I said, I didn't think that you did it. I'm just telling you what I heard."

"Okay, Miss I'm-not-Michael-Lawrence's-girl-friend," he said. "I'm just telling you that I didn't do it, and I don't know who did.

"You guys should get over that whole curse thing, anyway," he added. "It's so elementary school."

I couldn't help myself. I laughed out loud.

"Thanks for talking to me, Danny," I said sincerely. "If you think of anything I should know about the cougar incident, give me a call. And good luck with the football scholarship."

"Football?" He laughed. "I've got the highest average in my school. I'm not counting on something like football for a scholarship. It's just a game."

"Oh, then good luck with that academic scholarship," I said, trying to end the call before I got any more flustered. "And thanks again for talking to me."

"My pleasure," he replied. "See you at the field sometime. And if you ever want to watch the game from the winning side, come on down to West Hills for a game. You'll be my guest."

It felt like I was never going to be able to end the conversation, but we finally said our last good-byes and I hung up the phone. I looked at it, unsure who to call next. I had finished talking to everyone on Emma's list, and I really wanted to call Hailey and tell her all about the "Michael Lawrence's girlfriend" quote and about my odd, flirty conversation with Danny

Stratham, but I needed to keep my focus on the story.

I dialed a familiar number and waited for an answer.

"Hello, Mrs. Lawrence. This is Sam Martone," I said. "Is Michael around?"

"Sure, honey," Mrs. Lawrence replied. "Hold on a minute."

I heard a crash and bang and then a dial tone. Two seconds later, my phone rang.

"Is everything okay?" I asked, knowing that Michael would be on the other end of the line.

"Yes, just a little kitchen trouble." Michael laughed.

"Cougar Curse?" I suggested.

"Or my clumsy writing partner rubbing off on me," he joked.

I started to tell Michael all about my interviews with the West Hills kids and how annoyed they were that they were getting blamed for what happened to Mr. Cougar. I gave him a quick synopsis of each interview, but when I got to the last one, he interrupted me.

"Wait a minute. You talked to Danny Stratham?" he asked.

"Yeah, why?" I said. "I thought you said he was a good guy."

"Did I say that? I don't remember saying that," Michael replied. "What did *he* say?"

I wasn't about to tell him about the whole Miss Michael-Lawrence-is-not-my-boyfriend aspect of the conversation, especially when he seemed so miffed just because I talked to him, so I just said that Danny Stratham sounded nice and was easy to talk to.

"Nice in what way?" Michael asked. "Do you know he has a new girlfriend every other week?"

"I did *not* know that," I said. "I'll make sure to put it in the news report."

"Don't get wise with me, Pasty," Michael said. "It's just something I thought you should know."

"Okay, now I know," I said. "I think I'm finished reporting on my work. Let's hear about your interviews."

"I've been doing them," he said. "They've been going well."

"Feel like sharing any details?" I asked. "Who'd you talk to?"

"Just—just a few kids," he stammered. "You know most of them. We can go over it later. I just realized—I've got to get back to my cinnamon buns."

"All right, then," I replied. "I'll keep working on my end. Let me know if you find out anything interesting."

"Sure, Sam. Sounds good," he said, and then he hung up the phone abruptly.

★ ★ ★

Now I was ready to talk to Hailey. But when I called her house, her mom said she was at a meeting with Anthony Wright and the principal to talk about their plans for the school's student government team.

I finally got a chance to talk to Hailey when I got to school the next morning, but there were bigger things to discuss than boys. Officer Mendez and her partner were in Mr. Pfeiffer's office.

"What's going on?" Hailey asked. "This looks serious."

"I'm going to find out," I said. "Be right back."

I raced over to Mr. Pfeiffer's office and bumped into someone on the way. My books went flying all over the floor. When I looked up, Michael Lawrence was staring down at me.

"Cougar Curse, Pasty?" He chuckled.

"No, clumsy curse," I answered. "Help me. We have to talk to Officer Mendez and see if we can get the scoop."

Michael and I hovered around Mr. Pfeiffer's office until Officer Mendez walked out with Connor Bourke.

"Excuse me, Officer Mendez," Michael said. "We were wondering if there were any new developments in the case that we could report on."

"No new developments," she replied. "That's why we're here—to try to turn some up."

"Would we be able to sit in on your interviews and observe them?" I asked. "We wouldn't say a word."

"I'm sorry. I can't let you do that," Officer Mendez said. "That's confidential information."

"Is there any other information you *can* share with us?" Michael asked.

"We're trying to establish the timeline of the incident," answered Officer Mendez. "We also want to find out who might have been in the vicinity of the statue when the incident occurred."

"And you're doing that by interviewing students?" I asked.

"Yes, and also with other methods. The video cameras at the doors of the school didn't appear to capture anything, but we're still going to take a closer look at it. We also have data about which key cards were swiped to get in and out of the locker room before the game. Of course, that means we'll be interviewing the entire football team, including you, Mr. Lawrence. Care to join me in Mr. Pfeiffer's office?"

"What?" Michael said, stunned. "I mean, of course, I'm happy to answer any of your questions."

I watched as Michael sat down in the chair across from Mr. Pfeiffer's desk. His leg was shaking the same way it had in the police station. Officer Mendez started to close the door.

"See you later, Ms. Martone," she said. "Have a good day."

Hailey ran to catch up with me in the hallway on the way to class.

"Sam, why are the police talking to Michael Lawrence?" she asked. "That doesn't make any sense."

"It's not a big deal," I reassured her—and myself. "They're talking to everyone on the football team. It's standard procedure."

"Samantha Martone, when you talk to Michael Lawrence later and find out what happened in that office—and I know that you will—I had better be the first person you call," she said.

"I promise," I said. "You better be home to answer my call! I tried to get you yesterday and you were in some important meeting."

On the way to class, I told Hailey all about my phone calls with Danny Stratham and Michael Lawrence. She thought Michael's response was definitely a jealous reaction. I wasn't sure. He seemed more uncomfortable than jealous.

He seemed even worse at our *Voice* meeting that afternoon. He was back in his spot next to me on the love seat, which was a good sign, but

I could tell he was hardly paying attention to anything Mr. Trigg said at the beginning of the meeting.

When we broke off into teams, I asked him what happened in Mr. Pfeiffer's office with Officer Mendez.

"I can't tell you that, Sam," he said. "That's confidential information."

"Very funny," I said. "So what did you two talk about?"

"I'm not joking," Michael replied. "I can't tell you what we talked about."

"Michael Lawrence, we are working on an investigative report on the very incident that you were meeting with a police officer about in the principal's office," I reminded him. *Tell me what you talked about!*"

"Samantha Martone, do you remember Mr. Trigg's lecture about journalism and ethics?" Michael reminded me. "That would be blurring the lines."

"How?" I said angrily. "I don't see it. We need to use all of our resources to get to the bottom of the story, and you talking to the police about the incident is just one of those resources. As long as it's legal and ethical, there's no problem."

"Let me spell it out for you, then," Michael said, just as angrily. "I spoke to Officer Mendez as a member of the football team. Not as a reporter. I don't think it is ethical to share that information. *And nothing you say is going to convince me otherwise.*"

Whoa.

"I think our meeting's over now," Michael added. "See you around, Sam."

Then he stormed off.

I was so confused by what had just happened, I didn't know how to react. I think I had just yelled at Michael Lawrence. I think he had just yelled back at me. I think I'm still mad at him. And I think I'm even angrier because I don't like it when we disagree. We always see eye to eye on things. That's why we work so well together.

Mr. Trigg came over to the love seat.

"Is everything okay, Ms. Martone?" he asked.

"I'll be fine," I said. "Michael and I just had

a difference of opinion about how to approach the cougar story. We'll work it out."

"Ms. Martone, when I'm in a pickle, I try to picture someone I admire and imagine the way that they'd handle it."

"You mean like Winston Churchill?" I asked.

"Exactly!" Mr. Trigg beamed.

★　★　★

A thought about Mr. Trigg's advice all day, and I was still thinking about it when I went to bed that night. It was a pickle, all right. Who would compare to Winston Churchill as a mentor, though?

I looked out my window and saw a star. "Star light, star bright, first star I see tonight, I wish I may, I wish I might, have the wish I wish tonight." I have been doing that since I was really little. If you wish on the first star you see, your wish will come true. It's not a superstition either. It's just something you do. Before I closed my eyes to go to sleep, I made a wish. I wished that Michael Lawrence and I would get back to seeing things eye to eye. And I hoped that the Cougar Curse wouldn't get in the way of my wish.

# Chapter 7

## DYNAMIC DUO DISAGREES; MARTONE LOOKS FOR A QUICK FIX

★ ★ ★

My star wish didn't come true the next day. It proved my original point, though. Facts, you can count on. Wishes are as unreliable as curses.

Michael Lawrence avoided me like I had a bad case of the cooties. It was pretty easy for him to do that because Coach Dixon decided that the football team needed to double their practice time. Considering the outcome of the last two games, I couldn't disagree with his assessment. So I continued to gather information for the cougar story and figured that we'd work out a way to put it all together at our next *Voice* meeting.

My week also became a study in the "What would ____ do?" theory as I tried to put Mr. Trigg's advice to the test. *What would William Shakespeare do?* I thought in English class. *What would Alfred Wegener do?* I wondered in earth science. *What would Allie do?* I asked myself at home. Then I erased *that* thought from my brain. I could find a better mentor than Allie, for sure.

It turned out that Mr. Trigg had the answer in any case. I was sitting next to the newly silent and brooding Michael Lawrence at a surprise *Voice* meeting later that day.

"Ladies and Gentlemen," Mr. Trigg said, starting the meeting with his usual greeting. "It is my honor to introduce one of Cherry Valley's finest local reporters."

Who walked into the *Cherry Valley Voice* newsroom? Lauren Fields! Hello, mentor! What *would* you do?

"Salutations, journalists," Ms. Fields said to the *Voice* news team. "Let me start by saying thanks to Paul—I mean, Mr. Trigg—for inviting me here. And I'd also like to give a shout-out to Samantha Martone and Michael Lawrence. Hello, again, Sam and Michael!"

"Hello, Ms. Fields!" I chirped. "Great to see you again."

"Great to see you again," Michael said.

Mr. Trigg explained that Ms. Fields had come to Cherry Valley as part of her own investigation of the Mr. Cougar story, but that she had graciously agreed to join the *Voice* team meeting and was happy to answer questions and share advice with the students.

"Does anyone have a question for Ms. Fields?" Mr. Trigg asked.

The silence was excruciating, especially considering that we were supposed to be a group of inquisitive journalists. I felt Michael's leg start to shake and was surprised when he mumbled a question.

"I know you wouldn't put this in your news story," Michael said, "but if you had to guess, who do *you* think is responsible?"

"I'm sorry, Michael. I didn't hear all of your question," Ms. Fields said as she walked closer to the love seat. "Could you repeat it?"

"Do you have an idea who's responsible for the

vandalism?" Michael asked a little louder.

His leg felt like it was hitting the spin cycle on our washing machine.

"No, I don't," Ms. Fields said. "Of course, like everyone else, I thought the most likely suspects would be West Hills students. But I spent some time there, and I honestly haven't come across anyone that made my Spidey Senses tingle."

OMG! Ms. Fields just said Spidey Senses! She may not have been Winston Churchill, but she was definitely worthy of my admiration.

"Ms. Fields," I said. "I have a question that doesn't specifically relate to the cougar story."

"That's fine," she replied. "I'm here to answer all your questions."

"Great," I continued. "I was wondering what happens when an editor and a writer, or even two writers, don't agree on the direction of a story."

"That's a great question, Sam," Ms. Fields complimented me. "It happens every day at the *Gazette*, and I'm sure at every newspaper around the country.

"Most of us are raised to always think that

disagreements are a bad thing and full-blown arguments even worse," she continued. "But as a journalist, you need to grow a thick skin and get comfortable with the fact that not everyone will think the same way that you do. When we challenge each other, it always brings out the best stories. And I don't think that's true only for my profession either. It's a very good thing to develop the ability to listen to criticism objectively."

Ms. Fields went on to tell us a story that happened when she first started on the *Gazette*. She was working for an editor who had a reputation for being as hard as nails. He gave her small assignments, she turned them in, and he handed them back marked up with red ink. It was fine, because she knew she was just starting out and had a lot to learn.

Then one day, he gave her a chance to work on a bigger story. Ms. Fields poured her heart into the story and was extremely proud of her work. Ten minutes after she handed in the story, the editor returned it to her with a big red X on the front page. She wanted to cry. Then she got angry. A big red X wasn't going to help her become a better journalist.

Ms. Fields marched the editor's office and told him that. She said, "I know I can learn a lot from you, but I put my heart into that story and you just handed me a red X. That doesn't help me understand what you want."

"The problem *is* that you put your heart into it," the editor told her. "You're a journalist. Your heart shouldn't be involved in the process. You have to be objective at all times. On the other hand, you are absolutely correct about the red X. Let's talk about it and how to rewrite your story."

She finished by telling us that the editor sat down with her and went over her story line by line, explaining what worked and what didn't. Ms. Fields revised the story and the next day had her very first byline in the *Gazette*.

Everyone in the room clapped when she finished speaking.

"I know you have work to do too," she said. "So why don't you start your editorial meeting, and I'll just observe you in action."

"Thank you, Ms. Fields," Mr. Trigg said. "But please feel free to interject your thoughts during the meeting."

"Oh, I will." Ms. Fields laughed. "You can count on it."

We took turns giving updates to the stories we were working on, sharing information about the progress we were making and explaining any problems we were having. I had a lot to share—our meeting with Officer Mendez, my interviews with the West Hills students, my background research.

"Mr. Lawrence, do you have anything to add?" Mr. Trigg asked.

"Me? No, I think Sam mostly said it all," Michael replied. "I'm doing interviews too, but I haven't finished yet."

"Okay, Mr. Lawrence," said Mr. Trigg. "Just remember we have a paper to print, so wrap those up soon so you and Ms. Martone can turn in the story on time."

"Of course," Michael said, blushing.

When we split up into groups, Michael didn't have much more to say. "I'm sorry, Sam," he said.

"With the extra football practice and all, I just haven't had a lot of time to put into the interviews. But I'll wrap them up."

"That would be good," I said. "We really need to meet and start putting it all together, too."

"Yeah, sure," Michael said, but he seemed distracted.

I looked up and saw that Ms. Fields was walking over to us. Michael got up and shook her hand.

"Thank you, Ms. Fields," he said. "I learned so much from you. I have to run now. I have some interviews I need to catch up on."

Michael waved good-bye to some of the other kids in the room and darted off.

"Everything okay with you and Jimmy Olsen?" Ms. Fields asked.

"His name is Michael," I said, confused. "Michael Lawrence."

Ms. Fields laughed and explained that she was making a joke. Jimmy Olsen was a character who worked on the *Daily Planet* with Clark Kent, better known as Superman. I laughed along with her.

"Sorry," I said. "I knew that, actually. I'm

just a little off at the moment."

"Does Michael Lawrence have anything to do with that?" she asked.

"A little." I sighed. "Well, actually a lot. He's usually an excellent writing partner, and he always gets the job done. Lately he's been acting like the Cougar Curse is targeted at him. It's weird."

"That's tough," said Ms. Fields. "I can tell you two have great chemistry from reading the stories you've written together. You'll get it back. I know it."

"I hope so." I sighed again. "I'd like to do a great job on the cougar story. It's our first *real* news story."

"That's not really true, Sam," Ms. Fields said. "The news is whatever story is of high interest to your audience. Pay to play, healthy food for the cafeteria, school elections—those are all real news stories to the students at Cherry Valley."

"I never looked at it that way," I said, secretly smiling inside. "Thanks."

"One last piece of advice," Ms. Fields added. "Whatever Michael's problem is, it's *his* problem, not yours. You can always be his friend. You can be there for him if he needs you. But for now, focus on what you have to do. I know that's going to be hard. . . . He's really cute."

I knew my cheeks were probably as red as the inside of the cherry pie that was served for lunch that day in the cafeteria. "You think so?" I said, trying to sound casual. "He's all right, I guess."

Ms. Fields chuckled. "So, Martone, when are you coming to see me at the *Gazette*?" she asked.

"You were serious?" I said. "I'd love to visit."

"Have you ever been to a postmortem?" she asked. "That's when we review the stories we've written and talk about how we might do them differently the next time. I'll ask my editor, but I'm pretty sure he wouldn't have a problem with letting you sit in."

"I'd love to!" I gushed. "We don't really get a chance to do that here, because we only meet after school and we don't have a lot of time together."

"Perfect!" Ms. Fields replied. "Send me an e-mail to remind me to check into it. Sometimes I get so involved in a story, I forget about everything else."

"I know the feeling," I said. "I'll e-mail you as soon as I get home."

"I'll look for it in my in-box," she said. "Now I have to go interview some students for my story."

We shook hands good-bye and I started to pack up my stuff. Kids were trickling out of the newsroom, and it looked like the meeting was ending. On the way out, I stopped at my mail-box. There was an envelope marked CONFIDENTIAL. I knew those were my Dear Know-It-All letters from Mr. Trigg. I quickly stuffed the envelope in my book bag. Even though I was doing the bulk of the work on the Mr. Cougar story, I still had a Dear Know-It-All column to write too.

I knew I'd be home in a few minutes, but I couldn't wait to share my big news with someone. As soon as I got out of the school, I pulled out my cell phone and started to write a text.

Me: Mom! Guess who came to newsroom?


Mom: Who?

Me: LAUREN FIELDS!!!

Mom: Really?

Me: YES!!! And she asked me to come to a meeting at the Gazette.

Mom: That's incredible!

Me: I KNOW!!!

Mom: R u coming home?

Me: Be right there!

Mom: <3 u

Me: <3 u 2!

Mom was waiting at the door for me. She gave me a giant hug. "Tell me all about it!" she said. "I can't wait to hear."

I gave Mom a detailed description of every-thing that had happened at the *Voice* meeting. I was happy to relive every second of it!

"Is Michael going to the *Gazette* too?" Mom asked.

"I don't know. I was thinking of asking him, but . . ." I didn't know how to explain what I was feeling.

"Is everything okay between you two?" Mom asked.

"Oh yeah. It's nothing," I fibbed. "He's just a little busy with football. I'm not sure he'll have time to go."

"That doesn't sound like Michael," Mom observed. "He's usually so reliable."

"I know." I sighed. "It's the whole Cougar Curse thing."

"Don't tell me you believe in curses now?" Mom laughed.

"Never!" I said. "But I think everyone else in school does," I admitted.

"Sometimes it's easier to believe in myths than to recognize the truth that's staring you in the face," Mom said.

Mom had no idea how true her words were. By

Monday the Cougar Curse myth seemed to have taken over the school.

Mr. Rinaldi dropped his book at the beginning of math class.

"Oops, must be the Cougar Curse!" he joked.

"Don't joke about the curse," Sue Diaz gasped, "or it will come back to you ten times worse."

"Oh please," Bart Visitini said. "There's no such thing as a curse."

Finally! A rational thinker joins me at Cherry Valley Middle School.

"This is a good opportunity to review our ratio and proportion skills," Mr. Rinaldi said. "Let's take a vote. Who believes that the Cougar Curse is real?"

Sue raised her hand into the air and was joined by sixteen other students in the class.

"Who believes that the Cougar Curse isn't real?" Mr. Rinaldi asked.

Bart Visitini and I raised our hands. I looked around and was surprised to see twelve other kids had raised their hands too. I had obviously mis-calculated. There were more of us in the Cherry

Valley Rational Thinking Club than I had imagined.

"So what's the ratio of Cougar Curse believers to the total number of students in the class?" Mr. Rinaldi asked.

"Seventeen to thirty-one," Sue said after Mr. Rinaldi called on her.

"Correct," said Mr. Rinaldi.

"We are correct," Sue added. "Because the curse *is* real."

Everyone started calling out an opinion at the same time.

"Let's put math aside for the moment and discuss this," Mr. Rinaldi said.

"You just dropped a book," Bart said. "It happens all the time. Everybody drops a book so a curse had nothing to do with it."

"I have to agree with Bart's point," Mr. Rinaldi said. "Because I *have* dropped many books before Mr. Cougar was vandalized."

"What about all the other things that have happened?" Jordin Ali asked. "Our football team has never looked this bad before."

"Let's say the curse *is* real," Sue said. "How are we going to break it?"

"Well, if we're thinking about this logically—and I'm not sure that we are," Mr. Rinaldi said, "the logical answer would be that to break the curse, you would have to reverse the process that started it in the first place."

"So the Cougar Curse won't be broken until we fix Mr. Cougar?" Jordin asked.

"If you believe in the curse, I think that's your answer," Mr. Rinaldi replied. "Now let's get back to some ratios."

The word from math class started spreading around the school. Soon everyone was talking about plans to fix Mr. Cougar. They wanted the student government to get involved to make sure that the Cougar Curse was broken as soon as possible. I suggested they talk to Anthony and Hailey.

★ ★ ★

"Hey, Martone," I heard Hailey call as I stuffed my books into my locker before lunch period. "What's this I hear about Lauren Fields?"

"Can you believe it, Hails?" I said. "She

actually came to our *Voice* meeting. And she invited me to come to a postmortem!"

"What's that?" Hailey cried, alarmed. "At a morgue? Like where they have dead bodies?"

"Not a real postmortem, a *newspaper* post-mortem," I explained. "That's where the editors and writers and other staff from the paper meet to go over the latest issue and analyze it. They look at the things that were done well and the things that went wrong."

"That sounds right up your alley." Hailey laughed.

"There's actually a morgue at the *Gazette*, too," I said. "It's where all the old issues are kept. It used to be a room filled with file cabinets and actual copies of the paper, but today a lot of morgues are digital."

"Thanks for enlightening me," Hailey said. "I will never think of a newspaper in quite the same way."

"Did you hear about the plan to break the Cougar Curse?" I asked. "I think you and Anthony are going to be pretty busy."

"I know!" Hailey said. "I was nearly knocked over after gym period. A crowd of kids wanted to know what we were doing to fix Mr. Cougar."

"What did you tell them?" I asked.

"I was honest," Hailey replied. "I said that we hadn't done anything because we figured that the school would handle it. But if the students wanted us to get involved, we would bring it up to Mr. Pfeiffer."

"You're such a good VP," I said, proud of my best friend.

"You're such a good journalist," said Hailey, returning the compliment.

"I'd be a better journalist if my partner were pulling his weight," I said. "I'm going to have to pin him down in the cafeteria. I'll talk to you later."

"Good luck with that," Hailey said.

"Thanks. Even though I don't believe in luck, I'll take it now," I joked.

★　★　★

Michael Lawrence was scooping a pile of mac 'n' cheese into his mouth when I sat down next to him.

"Finished the interviews yet?" I asked.

"Almost," Michael answered.

"Got any interesting insights from anyone?" I asked.

"Not really," said Michael.

This was going worse than the time when I babysat my little cousin and he cried the whole time and wouldn't tell me what was wrong.

"Michael, we really need to get this story done," I said. "Today in math class we were talking about how you get rid of a curse. Maybe that would be a good angle to take."

"Sure. That's good," Michael said. "Better than trying to figure out who did it. I don't think we'll get very far with that angle."

"No, it doesn't seem like anyone is getting far with that angle," I agreed. "Even the professionals like Officer Mendez and Lauren Fields."

"Do you have any idea how to get rid of a curse?" Michael asked. "Because if I throw another interception, I might quit the football team."

"I don't have a clue how to get rid of something I don't believe in," I said. "But some of the kids in math class think that the Cougar Curse won't be broken until Mr. Cougar is fixed."

"Interesting," Michael replied. "I'll finish my interviews and ask some other kids what they think will end the curse. You can look it up on the Internet, too. Then we'll write the story about different ways to end the curse."

"Welcome back, Michael Lawrence," I said, smiling. "It's nice to have my partner back. That sounds like a good plan."

"I get it, Pasty," Michael said. "And I'm sorry. I just really have been feeling cursed lately."

"You could have told me that," I said.

"Next time, I will," he promised.

★  ★  ★

I was thrilled that Michael Lawrence and I were on the same page again, but that feeling didn't last long. Michael called me at home later that night.

"Hi, Sam. I have some bad news," he said. "It's going to cost thousands of dollars to replace Mr. Cougar. Mr. Pfeiffer said that we don't have the budget to do it. Maybe we shouldn't do the story about breaking the curse. If everyone believes that it won't be broken until Mr. Cougar gets fixed and he *never* gets fixed, Cherry Valley will be permanently cursed."

"I disagree," I said. "It's still a good story. It's what everyone's talking about. Real news is what matters to your audience. Our audience cares about the Cougar Curse."

"Do you mind if I talk to Mr. Pfeiffer first and find out the exact amount?" Michael asked. "I'll do it first thing in the morning."

"Okay. Just do it right away," I said. "We can't hold off on writing the story much longer."

# Chapter 8

## COUGARS HATCH A PLAN TO SAVE THE DAY

★ ★ ★

Obviously, Michael's talk with Mr. Pfeiffer didn't go very well. He showed up at my locker the next morning looking like the sullen Michael Lawrence I had been hoping had disappeared forever.

"It's going to cost five *thousand* dollars to fix Mr. Cougar," Michael reported. "Mr. Pfeiffer said the school can't afford to spend that much money on a statue."

"Five thousand dollars?" I asked incredulously. "It's not like Mr. Cougar's made of gold. That's a *lot* of money."

"Yup," Michael agreed. "Looks like the curse will continue."

"It *could* end right now if people stopped believing

in it," I replied. "The curse is ridiculous."

"Face it, Sam," Michael said. "That's not going to happen. You may not believe, but there are a lot of us who do."

"It looks like Mr. Cougar's going to be missing a paw for a while," I said. "So you might want to rethink that and just move on."

I didn't wait for Michael to answer. I had heard enough about the curse, and the bell for homeroom was just about to ring. I was really frustrated, too. How could someone with a brilliant brain like Michael believe in something as stupid as the Cougar Curse? It was mind-boggling.

Also mind-boggling were the letters to Dear Know-It-All. I opened them in the privacy of my room later that night—it was too dangerous to look at them in school and risk exposing my identity. I opened each letter, and they all sounded like they could have been written by the same person.

Dear Know-It-All,

Help! I've been cursed! I can't find my assignment pad anywhere.

-Looking for Luck

Dear Know-It-All,

Everything's been going wrong since Mr. Cougar's paw was broken. I don't know what to do. My dad yelled at me for my messy room. I'm so cursed!

-My Life's a Mess

Dear Know-It-All,

How long do curses last? Because I need the Cougar Curse to end right away. I have a math test next week and I don't want to fail another one.

-Math Cursed

I looked at the Dear Know-It-All e-mails that Mr. Trigg had screened for me, and they weren't any better. It was bad enough that Michael was giving me a hard time with the cougar story. I thought Dear Know-It-All might be the easy assignment this time around. I was obviously mistaken.

★    ★    ★

Michael looked a little more like his old self the next day at school.

"Hey, Pasty," he greeted me. "Did you hear the big news?"

"Nope, what happened?" I asked.

"I told Coach Dixon about the cost of fixing Mr. Cougar," Michael explained, "and that the school wouldn't be able to afford it. He had a great idea."

"What was it?" I asked.

"The team's going to try to raise some of the money ourselves," Michael answered. "We're going to have a fund-raiser."

"That *is* a great idea," I agreed. "How are you going to raise the money?"

"We thought a car wash would be fun," Michael said. "We can do it in the school parking lot. Coach said he'd even let us count it as a practice."

"Do what in the school parking lot?" Hailey asked.

Michael and I hadn't even seen her coming. Anthony Wright was by Hailey's side. Great timing, BFF—just when Michael Lawrence was beginning to seem like his old self for a minute.

"Hi, Anthony!" I said cheerfully. "Don't you and Hailey have some important school business to conduct?"

"Hi, Samantha," Anthony replied. "Actually, we do. Mr. Pfeiffer said that he wanted to talk to us about an important issue."

"It's probably Mr. Cougar," Michael told them. "The school can't afford to fix him. But the football team wants to have a car wash in the parking lot to raise money for the repairs. We won't get it all, but at least it will be a start."

"I like it," Anthony said. "I'll let Mr. Pfeiffer know that you have the support of the student government."

"I like it too," Hailey agreed. "I just wonder if there's a way to get more students involved. The

Cougar Curse doesn't just affect the football team, after all."

"Hailey's right," I said. "I know a lot of other kids who'd like the curse to end."

"What about a bake sale?" Anthony suggested.

"Perfect, partner," said Hailey. "Sam, we can make your Mom's Delish Dream Bars! I can smell them now!"

"Relax, Hailey," I said. "We don't even know if Mr. Pfeiffer will approve any of this yet."

Hailey gets a bit out of control when it comes to sugary snacks. Her mom's a bit of a health-food nut, and Hailey's dessert options usually consisted of a choice between fruit salad or trail mix.

"I don't think Mr. Pfeiffer will have an objection," Anthony said. "Hailey and I will bring it up to him in our meeting later. I'll let you both know if he gives it a green light."

"Thanks. I appreciate it," Michael said. "I'd do anything to stop the Cougar Curse."

"I'd do anything to get a bite of a dream bar." Hailey laughed.

"Well, I'd like to get a bite of a cinnamon bun,"

I added. "Any chance you'd make some for the bake sale, Michael?"

"Always thinking, Martone," said Michael. "I love that about you."

I couldn't look Hailey in the eye, because I knew she was thinking, *Ooooh, Michael Lawrence said* love*!* It did make my heart skip a little bit, but I didn't want *him* to see that.

★    ★    ★

The next day Mr. Pfeiffer didn't just approve the idea; he offered to wash some cars himself! The car wash/bake sale was going to be a big hit. Everyone wanted to see the principal get covered in soap bubbles, so they'd make sure their parents and every grown-up they knew would get to the event.

I had another big event to plan for too. Ms. Fields and I had exchanged a few e-mails, and I was going to the *Gazette* offices after school on Friday. I felt a little bad about not asking Michael, but he was kind of off on his own planet lately. Besides, Ms. Fields had invited me, not both of us. In any case, Michael probably didn't even want to go. But I was nervous, of course, about what to wear. As much as I hated to admit it, this situation called for a little Allie Martone advice.

I knocked on Allie's bedroom door on Thursday night.

"I'm *doing* my homework, Mom," Allie whined. "I swear I'm not texting!"

"It's not Mom; it's me." I snickered. "Can I come in?"

"If you must," Allie declared.

I opened the door to Allie's room and peeked inside. Allie had pulled her backpack onto her bed, just in case it had been Mom, but she had her phone in her hand and could barely make eye contact with me.

"Can you possibly be nice to me for five minutes?" I asked. "I know it's asking a lot, but it's been a tough couple of weeks."

"Cougar Curse getting to you?" Allie suggested.

"Something like that," I replied. "Tomorrow I have my big visit to the *Gazette*, and I don't know what to wear. Mom's picking me up right after school, so I don't want to stand out too much, but I do want to look professional and not like a kid at the meeting."

"Hmmm, sounds like a case for layering," Allie remarked. "Let's go take a look in your closet."

Allie pulled out a pair of navy blue leggings, a taupe long-sleeved T-shirt, and a pair of navy ballerina flats.

"This is what you're going to wear to school," she announced.

Then she shuffled through the closet and pulled out a dark chocolate–colored blazer.

"This is what you're going to keep in your locker," she continued.

She rushed across the hall to her room and returned with a patterned scarf. It had taupe, navy, and brown accents.

"This is what you're going to toss in your backpack," she declared. "Neatly folded, of course."

I tried the combination on and looked in the mirror. Allie was soooo good at this. I jumped up and gave her a big squeeze.

"You know, you're amazing sometimes," I admitted.

"Take it easy." Allie coughed. "It's just some leggings and a blazer. Get over it."

"Yeah, well, thanks," I mumbled. "Now you can get back to your . . . *homework*."

★ ★ ★

At the end of school on Friday, I grabbed my things and headed into the bathroom for a three-minute makeover. Blazer . . . check. Scarf . . . check. A nose for news . . . double check.

Mom was waiting for me outside of school with a bottle of water and a granola bar. "I know you don't want your stomach growling during a big news meeting," she said.

"Oh, that would be beyond embarrassing." I laughed. "It might even qualify as mortifying."

"I see you've been putting that vocabulary app to good use," Mom noted.

It took about a half hour to reach the offices of the *Gazette*.

"Are you sure you don't want me to come in with you?" Mom asked. "Just until you get situated?"

"I'm okay, really," I said. "Lauren Fields told me exactly what to do."

"And that is . . . ," Mom said, always looking for an opportunity to drill me on proper procedure.

"I go to the security desk. I show them my student ID. I tell them I have an appointment to meet with Lauren Fields. The security guard calls her. Then she comes down to meet me," I reported.

"Good girl," said Mom. "I'll be back in an hour. I know you said it will be longer than that, but if you need me earlier, just text me."

"I will," I said. "Do you think I look okay?"

"Better than okay, Sam," Mom said. "Like a professional."

I gave my mother a kiss and then followed the procedure I had described to her exactly. It took three minutes and twenty-seven seconds for Lauren Fields to come down after the security guard called her. I know because I counted every second. It helped to take my mind off of my nerves.

The newsroom was like a busy beehive. Phones rang in every corner of the room, reporters typed frantically on their keyboards, and small groups of people—I'm guessing editors and writers—argued vigorously. I couldn't tell exactly what they were saying, but I could see their hands flying through the air as they illustrated their points.

"It's a little crazy here," Lauren Fields commented. "I hope you don't mind."

"Mind?" I said. "I love it!"

"Good, because it will get even crazier in the meeting," she said. "Some people can get a little edgy when their work is criticized during a postmortem. Not me, of course, just some *other* people."

"I'm just so grateful to have the chance to sit in," I confessed. "I really can't thank you enough."

"You're welcome, Sam," Ms. Fields replied. "One day, you'll be the senior reporter taking a newbie for a tour. It's how we work in the news business, a lot of on-the-job training. There's only so much you can learn in school.

"Although don't get me wrong—school *is* important," she said, catching herself.

"Don't worry. I know," I assured her. "And if I

ever forgot, my mom would be sure to remind me."

Ms. Fields took me into a conference room with the longest table I had ever seen in my life. There must have been at least thirty chairs around it. Chairs also lined the outside wall of the room. Ms. Fields pointed to a chair in the corner.

"You can sit over there," she said. "Don't be nervous. I'm going to be sitting right in front of you at the table.

"If you need anything," she added. "Just kick my chair."

I sat down in the chair with my back as straight as a pin and my head held high, just like Mom had advised. I took out my notebook and pencil and watched quietly as the writers and editors entered the room.

Ms. Fields wasn't exaggerating. It took only about five minutes for the meeting to warm up. After ten, it was sizzling.

One reporter complained about the way his story had been cut to fill the news hole. I wasn't sure what that was, but Ms. Fields explained later that it was a term for the amount of space available in the paper. First the editors learned how much advertising had been sold for the day's paper. Then they figured out how big the news hole was. If there was a lot of advertising that day, and it seemed like there was on the day in question, then there was less space for the news.

I scribbled notes frantically. It felt like I could have filled up three notebooks with everything I observed in the meeting. I even had a few thoughts on how they could do things differently, but of course they were going to stay in my notebook. I could have fallen out of my chair, though, when Samuel Swope, editor in chief of the *Gazette*, turned his gaze in my direction.

"Ms. Martone, forgive me for not introducing you earlier," he said. "Ms. Fields has told me great things about you. Would you please tell the rest of the staff a little about yourself?"

I gulped, closed my notebook, and smiled nervously at the impressive and intimidating array of journalists seated around the table.

"Hello, everyone," I said. "Thank you so much for having me here today. My name is

Samantha Martone, and I'm a student at Cherry Valley Middle School. I work as a reporter on our newspaper, the *Cherry Valley Voice*, and it's my dream to one day be a real journalist, just like you."

One by one, the *Gazette* staff introduced themselves and gave me a sentence or two of advice. I could start a journalism textbook with their words!

Mr. Swope took control of the meeting again.

"Ms. Martone, as I'm sure you are aware, the newspaper business has been going through great changes in recent times," he informed me. "Some say it's a dying industry. We like to believe it's evolving. We also produce a Web version of the *Gazette*, and perhaps one day we won't print hard copies. I hope I don't get to see that day, though. I still love the smell of newsprint on my hands.

"With the future in mind, I'd love to get your take on the paper. We're always looking for ways to grow our audience, and if we don't appeal to the younger age group, then the people who predict that we're dying will be correct. So . . . any thoughts?"

I reopened my notebook and took a few seconds to get some things in my head that I thought were good enough to share. Then I cleared my throat. I heard my voice crack a few times, but you can't blame me. "I think that the local stories are really important," I said. "Especially the coverage of the schools and the sports teams, because that's the stuff we read, and I know those are the articles my mom reads too. We also rely on the newspaper to keep us up to speed on things that will affect us, like the school budgets or the new curfew at the park." In my wildest dreams I had never imagined that an entire table of journalists would be opening their notebooks to take notes about the things that I was saying! Incredible!

All the journalists looked friendly and a lot were nodding.

"Thank you!" said Mr. Swopes.

When the meeting had ended, everyone came over to me to shake my hand and wish me luck in the future. Lauren Fields was about to walk me down to the lobby when Mr. Swopes called out to her.

"Ms. Fields, Ms. Martone, may I interrupt for a minute?" he asked.

"Of course," Ms. Fields replied.

"Harry was telling me that you had an idea for the story about the Cherry Valley cougar," Mr. Swopes explained. "I'd love to hear your take on the story, and I'd like to get it wrapped up as soon as possible."

"I haven't fully fleshed out the story yet," Ms. Fields began, "but I thought I would write about the hyper-competitive nature of school sports these days and about how the crazed approach to competition led to the statue being vandalized."

"Interesting," Mr. Swopes said. "Do you have any evidence to prove that theory?"

"I've gathered quotes from players, fans, and parents about the increased pressure to compete," Ms. Fields replied.

"I'm not doubting that part of it," Mr. Swopes answered. "I'm just wondering how exactly you know that it led to the vandalism. Considering the police don't have a suspect yet. Or do you know something that I don't?"

"No, I don't," Ms. Fields admitted. "I'm no closer to knowing who did it than Sam is."

"Oh, Ms. Martone, do you have a lead on the story?" Mr. Swopes asked.

"Not one," I said honestly.

"Then I think you need to find a new angle, Ms. Fields," he declared. "Until we know who was responsible for the statue, that angle is pure speculation.

"Ms. Fields, sometimes a news story is just a news story," he continued. "No need to add drama to make it seem more interesting when it is already interesting at its core."

"I understand," Lauren Fields acknowledged. "I'll write a draft of the news story and get it to Harry right away."

"I look forward to reading it," Mr. Swopes said before walking away.

I couldn't believe Lauren Fields had gotten shot down like that, with me standing next to her, no less.

"If it makes you feel any better," I said, "I

thought your angle was a really good one."

"Me too." Ms. Fields laughed. "Seriously, though, he's right. Sticking to the simple approach may not seem like the most creative way to tell a story, but there are some stories that are just better when you let the facts tell them. They're the ones that usually lead to the investigative stories. Not every story can be a big dramatic one."

"Can you give me a minute while I write that down in my notebook?" I said. "That's an important lesson."

Ms. Fields and I chatted during the elevator ride down to the lobby. I went to shake her hand good-bye, but she gave me a big hug instead.

"Say hello to that cutie Michael Lawrence for me," she said as I walked toward Mom's car. "I hope things are working out better between you guys."

"Thanks!" I yelled back. "Me too!"

# Chapter 9

## COUGARS HATCH A PLAN TO SAVE THE DAY

★ ★ ★

Mom definitely had her listening ears on during the car ride home. I couldn't stop talking about everything that had happened in my visit to the *Gazette*. It was by far the most exciting day of my journalism career—maybe even my entire life!

Later I thought about Mr. Swopes's advice to Ms. Fields as I typed an e-mail to Michael.

Michael,

Forget about the curses and stuff. I think we should take a straight news approach to the cougar story. What do you think? We could work on it together at the fund-raiser tomorrow.

—Sam

I thought Michael might be busy with the guys from the football team, getting ready for the big car wash, but he was obviously not too busy to reply right away. This made me even happier than I already was, which was pretty ecstatic to begin with. What's happier than ecstatic? Jubilant? Euphoric? Elated?

Hey, Pasty,

Sounds like a good plan. You can come to my house after the fund-raiser. My mom will drive us.

—Michael

I was all set to flop onto my bed and rewind on the day's events, playing them like a movie in my mind. Then I remembered—Dear Know-It-All! I still had that column to write too.

I logged on to my e-mail and clicked through letter after letter about the Cougar Curse. Then I saw one that didn't mention the curse at all.

Dear Know-It-All,

If I know one of my friends did something wrong, how

do I handle it without feeling like a traitor? Should I tell someone? Do I keep my mouth shut? It was pretty bad, and I know he's sorry for what he did. He's just too afraid to tell anyone. I'm more twisted than a roller coaster.

Please help.

—Guilty Conscience

Whoa! That was heavier than I was expecting. I wondered if whoever wrote the letter knew who broke Mr. Cougar. This could be important. I opened a new file and started to type.

Dear Guilty,

Of course you should tell someone about what happened. You shouldn't even question it. If what your friend did was wrong, he or she needs to stand up and face the consequences.

—Dear Know-It-All

The doorbell rang, so I hit save and quickly closed the file. I didn't want anyone snooping around and finding out that I was Dear Know-It-

All. Hailey was coming over to make dream bars for the bake sale, and as hard as it was, I couldn't even let my best friend know about that assignment.

I was a little worried that we wouldn't have any dream bars left to sell. It seemed like Hailey was chowing down on them as fast as we could take them out of the oven. But even Hailey had her dream bar limit—eight, totally gross—so we wrapped up the rest of them and went to bed. Not to sleep, of course. Allie needed some payback for the squealfest she threw with her friends, so Hailey and I made sure to scream our loudest right in the direction of Allie's room as we watched not-so-scary movies that night.

★　　★　　★

When Mom pulled up at the school parking lot the next morning, there was already a line ten cars long waiting to be washed. And we were an hour early! Hailey and I ran to the bake-sale stand while Mom and Allie waited in the car.

The dream bars sold out in less than twenty minutes. It seemed like every parent at Cherry Valley and their friend pulled their car into the parking lot that morning. It was definitely worth the price of the car wash to see Mr. Pfeiffer in gym shorts and a T-shirt, totally soaked from head to toe. I wondered if Jeff Perry, the photo editor, had gotten a photo of that—who was I kidding? He probably had a whole camera full.

I was in the middle of selling half a cherry pie to Jenna and her dad when I saw Hailey waving frantically in my direction and pointing. I looked in that direction and saw that Danny Stratham was walking toward me. Yikes!

He waved at me and smiled. I could definitely see where he got the ladies' man reputation and why so many girls liked him.

"Samantha Martone, fancy meeting you here," he said, grinning.

"I go to school here, Danny, and you know it," I said, trying not to grin. "What's your excuse?"

"The guys from West Hills felt bad for the Cougars," he explained. "We like the competition. It's no fun to play against teams that are easy to beat.

"We talked some of our parents into getting their cars washed here," he added. "And I'm here to check out the snacks."

"And the girls?" Hailey coughed behind me.

"Oh, just one girl in particular," Danny said, winking at me.

I tried to ignore the wink.

"There's not many snacks left, so if you want something, you'd better choose now," I said matter-of-factly.

Just then, a soaking-wet Michael Lawrence came sloshing over to the booth. "The guys on the team are going to be hungry after this is done, Sam," he said. "So you'd better save some snacks for us."

I wasn't sure why Michael sounded so gruff when he said that, but I had an idea . . . and its initials were D.S.

"We already put some aside," Hailey told him. "Don't worry. Sam's thinking about you."

"Oh and, Sam," Michael said before he walked away. "My mom will be here in a half hour to pick us up. You *are* still coming to my house, right?"

"Right," I said. "I'll be ready."

Danny Stratham picked up a cupcake and handed me a dollar.

"Thanks for the snack, Samantha," he said. "You're still sure that's not your boyfriend?"

"I'm sure," I said. "We're working on a story together. The Cougar Curse story."

"Well, it would sure be bad luck for Lawrence if you found a new partner to hang out with." He laughed.

"Danny Stratham, that's enough!" Hailey interrupted. "We appreciate that West Hills is supporting our cause, but it's almost time for us to pack up. So thank you—and good-bye. Enjoy the car wash!"

"Thanks," I said to Hailey when Danny walked away. "I don't know why I have trouble getting out of those conversations."

"Um, let me see, cute . . . athletic . . . charming . . . I can't imagine why you'd want to talk to someone like that."

"I do *not* like Danny Stratham, Hailey," I protested. "You know that."

"I know you don't like him," Hailey countered.

"But you can like flirting with him. I'd wonder what was wrong with you if you didn't."

"He's not that charming." I laughed.

★   ★   ★

By the time we helped pack up the booth, Michael's mom had arrived to pick us up. Back at Michael's house, he set up the laptop in the kitchen so we could work side by side at the kitchen table. Danny Stratham who?

"I'd offer you a snack, but I'm guessing you're not very hungry," Michael's mom said. "I have some work to do, so I'll just get out of your way. If you do get hungry, just tell Michael."

"Thanks, Mrs. Lawrence. You're right. I'm totally stuffed with snacks," I said.

"You can start typing your notes into the laptop," Michael said. "I'm going to get out of these wet clothes. Be right back."

I started by typing the basic questions that are crucial to every good news story.

Who?
What?
Where?

When?

Why?

We didn't know "Who" or "Why" yet, but I had at least a little info to fill in for the rest of the questions.

Michael returned in some dry sweatpants and a T-shirt. He sat down next to me, smelling like soap and car wax. I liked it. I didn't like the way he was acting, though. He wasn't quite sullen Michael, but he was definitely worried or bothered by something. I hoped it wasn't me, but I wasn't really sure.

Our story turned out just like our work session— good, solid, but not very exciting.

# Chapter 10

## THE TRUTH IS REVEALED

★ ★ ★

My work as Dear Know-It-All gave me a lot of insight into the emotional lives of my fellow students at Cherry Valley Middle School. It did not prepare me, however, for the phone call I received that night.

"Hello, Sam?" I heard a shaky voice say on the other end of the line.

"Michael? Is that you?" I asked.

"Yes," he said. "I have a confession to make. I've been keeping something from you."

"Okay, what is it?" I said. "We're friends. You can tell me anything."

"Are you sure?" he asked. "Anything?"

"I'm sure, Michael," I answered, starting to feel impatient. "Just say it."

"You know how I wasn't really telling you

about the interviews I did with the Cherry Valley kids?" he asked.

"I know. You never did the interviews," I said. "You were busy with football practice and the stupid Cougar Curse. It's okay. I understand."

"No, Sam, that's not it!" said Michael, sounding less shaky. "I did the interviews. And I found out who broke Mr. Cougar."

"Michael Lawrence, are you kidding me?" I was stunned.

"I'm not joking, Sam," he answered. "I'm dead serious."

"You just sat right next to me for hours working on this story, *and you didn't mention that you know who did it*!" I yelled.

"*I know!*" he yelled back. "I feel terrible. That's why I'm calling."

"So what, you wanted to keep the scoop all to yourself?" I asked. "Get a front-page byline of your own?"

"Come on, Sam. You know me better than that," Michael replied. "It's not like that at all. It's not what anyone thinks at all."

"What is it, then?" I wondered.

"It wasn't the guys from West Hills, Sam," Michael explained. "It was kids from Cherry Valley. It was supposed to be a prank. They wanted to put underwear on Mr. Cougar. They thought it would make everyone laugh before the game. But when they started to get the underwear on, the statue tipped over.

"They panicked," he added. "That's when they decided to make it look like someone vandalized the statue."

"Michael, you heard Officer Mendez," I said. "This is a crime. You need to tell someone what you know, even if some of these people are your friends."

"But I'd feel like such a traitor, Sam!" he cried. "I hang out with some of these guys every day! They're my buddies."

"It doesn't matter," I answered. "There's only one right thing to do. So do it."

"You're not listening, Sam," Michael pleaded. "These guys are my friends. They didn't mean to do it. And they're really, really sorry.

"That's why we came up with the idea to do the

fund-raiser," he explained. "We figured it would be a good way to come up with the money to fix Mr. Cougar. Then everything would be okay."

I stopped and thought for a moment. Was I better than the guys who broke Mr. Cougar? A few months ago, I picked some flowers on my way home from school with Hailey. I went to put them in my mom's favorite vase to surprise her. But the vase slipped and crashed into a million pieces on the floor. I didn't want to get in trouble, so I swept up the pieces and threw them in the neighbor's trash can so Mom wouldn't see them. Mom's been looking for that vase for months. It hurts my heart every time I see her digging through a box or pulling stuff off a closet shelf. I was hoping she'd forget about it, but she hasn't. So I guess I'm just as guilty as the Cougar vandals, after all.

I decided to be a real friend, and I shared my story with Michael.

"So you kind of know what I mean?" he asked, sounding a little hopeful.

"Kind of," I answered. "But not really. Breaking a vase is an accident. Vandalizing something is a crime even if it started as an accident. I still think you should tell. But I understand why you don't want to."

"Thanks for listening, Sam," Michael said. "I'll definitely think about what you said."

"I hope you do," I replied. "See you Monday at school?"

"See you Monday at school," Michael said before hanging up.

★   ★   ★

I tossed and turned in bed that night. I felt like a hypocrite. What would Winston Churchill do? What would Lauren Fields do? What would *I* do?

# Chapter 11

## DEADLINE APPROACHING FAST; MARTONE HUSTLES TO MEET IT

★ ★ ★

I sent Lauren Fields an e-mail before I went to school on Monday. She replied right away and said I should call her after school.

The day seemed endless. I usually enjoyed my classes more than most of my classmates, but I felt like I was locked up in a cell that I couldn't escape from. Mostly I felt like I was locked up in my own brain and I wanted to escape from that. I didn't know what I would do if Michael didn't tell someone what he knew. I didn't know how I could let the broken vase cover-up go on. I wanted it all to just go away.

I could tell Michael was feeling the same way, although he didn't have much to say to me that day. We passed each other in the hall on the way to the cafeteria. We both nodded and then put our heads down.

"What's up with you?" Hailey asked. "Wait a minute. . . . Is it Danny Stratham again?"

Trust Hailey to make a girl laugh in her darkest hour.

"No, it's not him," I said. "It's just this story we're working on. We're . . . we're having trouble putting all the pieces together."

"Well, it's not going to come together if you just nod your heads and don't talk to each other," Hailey noted.

"I know. You're right," I agreed. "We just need some time. Trust me. It will all be okay."

"I know it will," Hailey said. "You guys are the dynamic duo of the *Cherry Valley Voice*! How could it not turn out okay?"

I hoped that Hailey was right. That afternoon I waited on the love seat during the *Voice* meeting, but the seat beside me sat empty. Michael rushed into the meeting fifteen minutes after it started. I nodded at him, but this time, he didn't make eye contact. He just sat in that same chair in the back of the room, and then he left fifteen minutes early.

I went home and made my call to Lauren Fields. I told her that Michael knew something about what happened to Mr. Cougar and that he knew the people who were responsible for damaging the statue, but that he wasn't ready to share what he knew.

"Wow, that's a tough one," she said. "It's pretty impossible to be neutral when you know the people involved in a story. He should tell what knows because it's the right thing to do. Then he should take himself off the story. He's just too close."

I knew she was right, but I had no idea how I was going to convince Michael to do that. Luckily, I didn't have to.

Michael called later that night, sounding even worse than he had during our previous conversation.

"Sam, I just wanted to let you know that I talked to Coach Dixon and Principal Pfeiffer," he said.

"You did?" I said incredulously. "I'm so glad you called them. What did you say?"

"I told them everything I knew," he stated. "And I felt like a traitor the whole time."

"I'm sorry. That must have been so tough," I said.

"It was," Michael confessed. "And it turns out they'd already suspected the kids who did it. They said they appreciated my honesty. They also promised to keep my name out of the investigation."

"That's good news," I said, trying to be cheerful. "Right?"

"Sure. No one will know I'm a traitor but me," Michael answered sarcastically.

"You're not a traitor," I assured him. "You did the right thing."

"There's another thing I have to do to make things right," Michael added.

"What is it?" I asked.

"I don't think I can work on this story with you," he announced.

"I agree," I told him. "You're too close to it to

be objective. I understand."

"Thanks," he said.

"See?" I said. "You did two right things in one day. You shouldn't feel bad."

"Right," said Michael. "I ratted out some of my friends, and I let my favorite writing partner down. Best day ever.

"Oh, and I still have the Cougar Curse," Michael added. "I threw four interceptions in practice today."

"Well, Mr. Cougar will be fixed soon, and then the curse will be lifted," I said hopefully. "Just see if you can wait it out a little longer."

"Thanks, Pasty," Michael said. "I'll try."

★    ★    ★

After I hung up the phone, a wave of guilt rushed through my body. Michael Lawrence had been brave enough to tell the truth. What was my problem?

I went into my mom's room and sat at the edge of her bed. "Mom, I have something I need to tell you," I said solemnly.

"What is it, Sam?" she asked. "Bad grade?

Missed an assignment? Trouble with Hailey?"

"No, none of those things," I answered. "I did something really bad a few months ago, and I hid it from you. And I'm really so sorry that I didn't just tell you right away."

Mom put her hands down on the bed, as if she were trying to prop herself up. I didn't know what was going through her mind, but I don't think it was a broken vase.

"What did you do, Sam?" she said, her voice almost as low as a whisper.

"I broke your favorite vase—you know, the blue one with the white flowers," I said. "I didn't mean to, Mom. It was a complete accident. I was actually trying to do something nice for you. I picked you a bunch of wildflowers and I was going to put it on the kitchen table. It just slipped out of my hand."

Mom looked relieved. Then she looked serious again. "I know accidents happen," Mom said. "But that vase was from Grandma. It can never be replaced."

I felt hot tears stream down my cheeks. I hated

breaking Mom's vase, but I hated hurting her feelings even more. I didn't know what to say.

"There's another, even more important thing that's very hard to replace when you break it, Sam," Mom added. "Do you know what it is?"

"No," I admitted.

"It's trust," Mom said. "It hurts that you broke that vase, but I would have gotten over it. It hurts even more that you hid it from me. You broke a piece of our trust, Sam, and that's a really delicate thing."

By now I was pretty much bawling my eyes out. "Will you ever trust me again?" I wailed.

Mom pulled me close, hugged me, and gave me a kiss on the top of my head. "Samantha Martone, you are a good girl," she said. "I know that, and I trust you. So let's keep it that way. If you do something wrong and you tell me, that trust will stay strong."

"I promise, Mom." I sniffed. "I will never ever keep anything from you again."

"I hope so," Mom said. "And you'll make up the broken vase by folding laundry for a month, deal?"

"Deal," I agreed.

Mom and I shook hands; then we hugged each other tightly.

"Mom?" I said.

"What is it, Sam?" she asked.

"I just remembered something really important I need to do," I explained.

"Okay, so go do it!" Mom laughed.

My Dear Know-It-All column draft was waiting on my computer. It needed a major rewrite.

★ ★ ★

I woke up the next morning and found a message in my e-mail in-box.

Sam,

Just wanted to check in and see how everything went.
I believe in you.

—Lauren Fields

I picked up the phone and called the *Gazette*. I wasn't sure if Ms. Fields would be at work so early, but I figured that since she was a reporter, she probably got an early start. I was right.

"Hi, this is Sam Martone," I said. "I got your e-mail. Thanks for thinking of me."

"Hi, Sam," Ms. Fields replied. "How are you? What's going on?"

"I was just wondering if you ever use confidential sources," I asked. "You know, off the record?"

"All the time, Sam," Ms. Fields said in a serious reporter tone.

"Well, then, this confidential source is informing you that they know who did it, and it's not the kids from West Hills," I reported, feeling like I was in the middle of the Watergate investigation.

"Thanks so much, Sam," Ms. Fields said. "I'm on it!"

★    ★    ★

She wasn't kidding, either. The next day the story hit the *Cherry Valley Gazette*.

### Cougar Cursed by Prank Gone Bad

The story went on to inform the readers that kids from Cherry Valley were responsible for the damage to the cougar statue in front of Cherry Valley Middle School. It didn't name names, but all the details were in there. I admired Ms. Fields's work. The story was straightforward but factual. As Mr. Swopes said, "Sometimes a news story is just a news story."

I tried to take that advice as I finished my story for the *Voice*. I interviewed Mr. Pfeiffer and Officer Mendez and typed in some final revisions quickly, the clock ticking over my shoulder.

*They are withholding the names of the students at the present time, but "They know who they are, and we know where they are," said Officer Mendez. "We're working with their families to determine the best way that they can pay the restitution needed to repair the statue."*

*A confidential source has informed this reporter that the students are incredibly sorry for their actions and feel terrible about covering it up.*

I saved my final draft and sent it to Mr. Trigg for approval. Then I left the newsroom and looked for Michael. I found him outside the locker room.

"Hey, is everything okay?" I asked as I approached him.

He smiled at me, a bright, beautiful, happy smile that I had really, really missed.

"Getting better all the time," he said.

"Coach Dixon just gave the team a big talk," he added. "He talked about the importance of being honest and owning up to your mistakes. It worked. The kids involved in the Mr. Cougar incident stood up and admitted that they did it!"

That was newsworthy information! I wondered why Mr. Pfeiffer hadn't shared it with me during the interview. Good thing I had a reliable inside source on the story: Michael Lawrence!

"Oh, and one other thing," Michael continued. "The kids have agreed to get after-school jobs. They're going to help pay for the repairs. They're also going to be suspended from most of our future games."

"I'm sorry," I said sincerely. "That has to hurt."

"I won't lie. It does," Michael confessed. "I don't think we're winning the championship anyway this year, though."

"I'll admit, it doesn't look that way," I agreed. "But look on the bright side. There's so much room for improvement now!"

Michael reached over and ruffled my hair. I thought I felt a spark, but I wasn't sure if it was just that static electricity thing that happens, or something else.

# Chapter 12

## ALL'S WELL THAT ENDS WELL

★ ★ ★

Nearly all the students in the hallways of Cherry Valley Middle School had their heads in a copy of the *Voice* after it was distributed at the end of the week. The headline of my story, **Cougar Curse Cracked**, appeared in big, bold letters at the top of the fold.

"That's surprising," I said as I turned to Hailey and snatched the paper from her hands. "It's old news already. The story's been out for a few days. Why is everyone so interested in it now?"

"It's been out, but everyone knows that you're the source for the real facts," Hailey explained. "And don't look like you don't know that, either. You can feel proud, Sam. You did a great job."

"Thanks, Hailey," I said. "I really do feel proud."

"It's an important story. There were so many rumors and interpretations going on," Hailey added. "Sometimes you just need the plain black-and-white facts."

I had never agreed more with my best friend.

We plopped into our seats in homeroom and listened to the announcements made by Principal Pfeiffer over the PA system.

"Students, I have some incredible news to share with you today," Mr. Pfeiffer told the school. "And anonymous donor has volunteered to fix Mr. Cougar. He or she will put up the money to pay the bill until the students can pay back the amount. The Cougar Curse is lifted!"

Homeroom is supposed to be a silent period, but every classroom in the school erupted with cheers after Mr. Pfeiffer's announcement. You would have thought the Cougars had won the championship game or something, not that some silly curse was broken.

I was walking home from school that afternoon when Michael Lawrence caught up to me.

"Mind if I walk with you?" he asked.

"Not at all," I said. "You're just going a little out of your way, you know."

"I know." He smiled. "I need the exercise. Gotta get ready for the next football game.

"Great job on the cougar story, Pasty," he added. "I'm sure Lauren Fields is proud of you. I know I am."

"Thanks," I said.

I turned my head to the side just in case I was blushing a little. But Michael didn't notice, because he was pulling something from his backpack. It was the latest issue of the *Voice*.

"I also really liked the Dear Know-It-All column," he said. "I mean, listen to this. . . ."

I like to think of what someone I respect would do. It's always tempting to think you can get away with something or try to cover it up and make it better, but the truth usually comes out, and in the meantime, it will eat you up inside and twist you around like a roller coaster. Being honest is always the best policy. It sounds boring, but sometimes the most straightforward approach is the best approach. No one ever regrets doing the right thing, but doing the wrong thing can really haunt you.

"That's pretty good advice," I said.

"I think so," Michael agreed. "I definitely know what it's like to be twisted like a roller coaster. And I was sure Dear Know-It-All would know the right thing to do."

I twisted up my face, squinted my eyes, and looked at Michael sideways. Wait a minute! Did *he* write the letter? Did he know that *I'm* Dear Know-It-All?

"Dear Know-It-All is definitely a smarty," I said, trying to stifle a giggle.

"She is," Michael replied. "It's a great idea to think what someone you respect would do."

Did you ever have a moment with someone when you feel like time just stops and stands still? Not like one of those romantic scenes in a movie, where the winds are blowing and you're staring into each other's eyes dreamily. Just a sort of *Wow, we're so in sync and everything feels so right; let's just stop and stay quiet and enjoy it all* kind of a moment? That's the moment I had with Michael Lawrence just then.

Of course, then we both burst out laughing a few moments later.

Then Michael raised his water bottle into the air and proposed a toast. "Here's to doing the right thing," he said.

I clinked my water bottle to his.

"And to being rid of the Cougar Curse!" I added, right before the bottle slipped out of my hand and I spilled water all over myself.

"But never being rid of the Clumsy Curse!" Michael laughed. "That's my favorite curse ever!"

★     ★     ★

That night, before I closed my eyes to go to sleep, I looked out my window and tried to find my lucky star. I didn't see it, but I thanked it anyway.

# Extra! Extra!

Want the scoop on what Samantha is up to next?

Here's a sneak peek of the eleventh book in the Dear Know-It-All series:

## Late Edition

# SUBURBAN TEEN DIES OF SLEEP DEPRIVATION!

★ ★ ★

I rolled over and stared at the clock next to my bed. The numbers cast a bloodred glow across both the computer and the empty diet cola can on my bedside table. It was 1:05 a.m. I quickly did the math in my head for the tenth time that night: My alarm will go off at 6:15, which means if I fall asleep *right this very second*, I will still get only five hours and ten minutes of sleep.

Which is not enough.

I sighed heavily and flopped on my back to stare at the ceiling. I'd read an article a few months ago on Huffington Post about teenagers and how their internal clocks are out of whack with the rest of society. I guess a lot of studies have been done and teenagers' bodies need to stay up late and sleep late. (Like I did this morning. Blissful eleven-o'clock Sunday-morning sleep-in!) It's some kind of adaptation that has developed over thousands of years. Maybe I should pitch an article to Mr. Trigg, our school newspaper advisor, on teenage sleep patterns. That could be good. I flipped on my lamp, wincing at the brightness, and reached for my laptop to e-mail the idea to myself. (My trusty notebook was already packed in my messenger bag and I didn't feel like getting up to get it.) After closing the computer, I switched off the lamp and settled back under the covers with a sigh, waiting for sleep to come. I sighed again loudly and fluffed my pillow. Nothing.

**Suburban Teen Dies of Sleep Deprivation!**
I wondered how fast it could happen.

At some point I must've fallen asleep, but it was well after one thirty, because that was the last time I remember doing my sleep math.

★　★　★

"Sammy, sweetheart, you're going to be late if you don't get up right now!" My mom sounded stressed.

"Yeah, sweetheart!" sang out my sister, Allie, passing by my room—while texting, I'm sure.

I groaned and thought about how I keep meaning to wear clean school clothes to bed so all I have to do is roll out and brush my teeth. Tonight. For sure.

"Just put your feet on the floor. Once you're up and moving, it will be a whole lot better. I promise," said my mom, watching me with folded arms from her perch in the doorway.

I did as she said and mentally reviewed my day, trying to figure out the soonest moment I could get some shut-eye, even if it was just a nap in the library.

"Okay, Mom. I'm up and it's not better!" I called, but she had already left.

★    ★    ★

My mom was a little bit right, in that once my day was under way, I wasn't as tired as I'd been all snuggled under my down comforter. Getting up in the morning is kind of like writing on deadline. You dread it, and it's hard to get started, but once you get going, everything just flows. That's how it is for me anyway.

Hailey and I were at lunch when I suddenly let out a huge yawn.

I wish I could have my day start later. I can't get to sleep at night, and it's driving me crazy!"

"Why?" asked Hailey, picking up a muffin from her tray and chewing thoughtfully.

"Well . . . it all started with midterms. I had two huge exams and an article, and I stayed up late a bunch of nights in a row, and it was like my body got adjusted to this new time clock and then I couldn't reset it."

"Huh," said Hailey with a shrug. "I never have any sleep problems. I pass out at night and pop up at the same time every morning. I don't know why. Sleep has never been an issue for me."

"Well, you're lucky," I grouched.

"Who's lucky?" asked a husky voice over my shoulder.

My ears tingled. My heart raced. It was Michael Lawrence, the one true love of my life.

"Hey," I said coolly, revealing nothing of the drama going on inside my heart.

"Ready to go to the meeting?" he asked.

"Duty calls," I said in a resigned voice, standing up and gathering my things.

A voice came from the other direction. "Hey, Hails. Mind if I join you?"

I looked up. It was Molly Grant, a seventh grader I know a little. I felt immediately better. At least now I wouldn't be leaving Hailey at the table all alone.

But Hailey jumped up. "Uh, sorry . . . ," she muttered. "We were just leaving."

As Hailey fell into step next to me on our way to deposit our lunch trays, I said quietly, "What was that all about? Where do you need to be?"

"Molly copies me constantly! I wear red high-tops; she shows up the next day in brand-new red high-tops. I cut the sleeves off a T-shirt and layer it, and she does the same the next week. It's driving me insane!"

I glanced at Michael, who was waiting in the cafeteria doorway. He was chatting with Kate Bigley, whom I always worry he secretly likes.

"More on this later. Gotta go. Sorry," I said.

"Okay, bye." Hailey sighed. "Good luck."

I smiled and raced off.

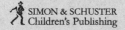